ZO|

MW00943299

Meowrrrr!

Dana Trantham

Wayward Cat Publishing

ZOMBIE CATS

CHAPTER ONE

After Busby died the third time, I started to get suspicious. But it wasn't until after he died the fifth time that I saw our neighborhood for what it was—a trap. We lived in a deadly, sheltered box, hemmed in by a deep, wide canal on the east, two four-lane roads, north and west, and a nine-foot tall wood fence on the south. We could easily be confined when they came to quarantine us. Did I really want to be penned up in a four-street neighborhood all summer with Sarah Johnston and Natalie Hunt? I wasn't sure how many cats would have to die, but I was sure I didn't want the FBI or NASA coming in with gas masks, imprisoning me with nobody but The Twits to talk to. Not that I have anything against The Twits. But I had bigger, better plans for the summer.

The first time Busby croaked, we had six weeks left until Rudy and I graduated from the sixth grade—don't get me started on elementary school graduation; I saw what they did to my cousin Lennie last year when he graduated high school. They put him in a purple dress! And he had to wear this flat hat on his head with a tassel dangling down in front of his face. When he and all his classmates threw their hats off at the end, I figured I'd have thrown my hat away, too. But Lennie picked his up again and brought it home, maybe to remind him of the humiliation he'd been forced to endure. I told Rudy the very next day that he'd never catch Alfie Whitaker in a dress. And Rudy, who does just about everything I do, said he wouldn't wear one either.

Rudy didn't say anything to The Twits at the bus stop that Monday morning. I didn't notice anything different about him because about the time he arrived at the corner of Manatee and Sand Hill, Brian Watley's car raced down Sand Hill and skidded to a stop at the stop sign.

Rudy's brother, Grant, hung out the front passenger window. "Hey little twits," he called.

Natalie rolled her eyes and sighed. "He's such a dweeb."

I wasn't paying attention to the dweeb. I was staring at the Alien, bending down to look out the passenger window at us, his thick, dark-rimmed glasses the only defining feature of his face.

I admit it. I was afraid of Brian Watley. We all were, but maybe me the most. We called him Alien Watley when he wasn't around. If he stared at you long enough you had to run away; some kids ran away crying. We'd all heard the stories about him dunking kids under the water in the ditch and throwing them off the second floor of the mall. I heard he threw a kid through a glass window. We never knew what to say to him because we didn't know what would set him off. His temper was legendary and I didn't ever want to see it. So we never said anything.

"See ya, twits," Grant called as Brian pulled the car out onto Manatee and took them away to the high school.

I was thinking how glad I was that it would be two more years before I joined them there. I just knew the school was filled with Brian Watleys–older, scary, staring at you, smarter than you, and laughing at you. I guess those were the things that scared me the most. Dead cats? *Nah.*

Rudy didn't say anything about Busby on the bus ride to school, either; he waited to tell us the story at lunch. Busby was hit by a car on Saturday, he said, and flew thirty feet to land squat on the sidewalk in front of Rudy's house. Orange and white fur flew everywhere, he said, and rained down in the road like feathers from a strange bird–his words, not mine. I could tell he'd been practicing his story. I was going to tell him he should use it in a poem for English class, but I thought I should show some respect for Busby's demise. I'd tell him that later.

Rudy buried Busby in the back yard with a little funeral and everything; but the next morning the cat was meowing at the back door, having clawed its way out of the shoe box and a foot of dirt. Of course I didn't believe him. If it had really happened, he'd have invited me over for the funeral. It's true I was at my grandmother's all weekend, at the beach condo. But I knew if it really happened, Rudy would have waited for me.

The second time, Rudy figured Busby ate a poisoned mouse because, he said, he hacked for five hours straight and all kinds of tiny body parts came out and then Busby keeled over on the back porch by the pool and stopped moving. Rudy didn't get a chance to bury him that time.

He held a wake in his back yard and I was invited because I'm his best friend, and probably because I told him why I didn't believe him about the first time. Brian Watley got to go too, on account of he's Grant's best friend. Or it could have been just because he was over that day. Rudy's dad and mom and gram were there, and Rudy made them all go out back, again, by the pool where Grant and Brian had re-dug the hole against the back fence.

Standing poolside, next to a TV table with Busby's shoe box on it, we all took turns remembering the things we liked about Busby. He looked like he was sleeping, not peacefully though; you could tell he'd been hacking up a dead mouse when he hit The Big One.

Rudy's mom said, "Well, here we are again. I hope you're really dead this time." And his dad said, "Sorry about burying you and all, last time." Rudy's brother Grant poked him with a stick. I said how much I liked it when Busby brought me dead lizards in his mouth whenever I was over at Rudy's, even though he growled at me if I tried to take them. When Rudy's gram stood up and said she really couldn't think of anything nice to say, Busby sneezed and lifted his head up out of the box to look around at us all.

Chapter Two

udy's mom screamed and knocked over some of the chairs trying to get inside the house and Rudy's gram nodded triumphantly. I guess rising from the dead was another bad mark against Busby. Don't tell, but I agree with Rudy's gram. Busby was not the nicest cat in the neighborhood.

The third time, Rudy came to school weepy and said Busby was dead again. This time it was for sure because he was flat as a flour tortilla. That very morning, Busby was sleeping on top of the old refrigerator out in Rudy's garage when Rudy and Grant were fighting over the red baseball cap again. Rudy swears the cap is his because he found it in the street in Orlando last summer—his mom washed it for him in this really strange, plastic, hat cage. But Grant says it's his, that he bought it at the mall. Nobody knows, but I'm pretty sure the hat Rudy found in Orlando was brown.

Anyway, Grant shoved Rudy up against the refrigerator in the garage, and, because it was empty with the door chained shut, and off balance, it started rocking forward and back. Rudy said Busby made a howling kind of noise from on top of it, probably annoyed, but he didn't pay much attention as he pulled away from Grant and grabbed hold of the door handle. Grant pulled Rudy, and Rudy pulled the refrigerator over. It was lucky, I said, not giving Rudy the sympathy he wanted, that the fridge didn't fall on him and Grant, because then they'd be flat.

Rudy glared at me. "My mom said the same thing."

"She was right," I said.

"But Busby's flat as a spit splat. My mom didn't even believe me when I told her Busby was under there. She just yelled at me to get my dad to pick the fridge up. And the fridge landed on a pile of her groceries and they were smashed and thrown across the floor so she wasn't paying any attention about Busby."

Rudy said it took his father and Grant and Mr. Haggarty from next door, to lift the refrigerator off Busby. Mr. Haggarty slipped on the garage floor and got oil on his best suit pants and cursed all the way home. It wasn't car oil, because the Albees never put their cars in the garage. It was cooking oil. One of Mrs. Albee's bottles of cooking oil leaked. The point is, nobody but Rudy paid any attention to poor dead Busby.

"Flat as a spit splat," I said, and probably shouldn't have. "Say that ten times fast."

Rudy was not amused.

Busby was for sure dead this time. Still, I followed Rudy home from the bus stop that afternoon to see how dead he really was, but Busby was alive again and waiting for Rudy in the front yard.

And that's when I got suspicious. It was all the dying and living again, for one thing. And for another, it was the red in the eyes. Busby's eyes all of the sudden had this sort of pinkish glow to them.

"What's wrong with his eyes?" I asked Rudy.

"What? I don't see anything."

"Come on," I said. "They're red. Okay. Pink."

"That's just the sun."

We stood on the sidewalk in front of the house, right about the spot where Busby had lain crumpled and broken after the car accident, so Rudy said, and watched Busby. The cat just sat there in the yard, staring at us. He meowed.

"Okay, now that's weird. You gotta admit, that's weird."

"What?" Rudy said. "He's a cat. Cats meow."

"Not like that, they don't."

Busby had let out this long, haggard, once dead now alive kind of meow. It reminded me of my great grandmother when she slammed her hand in the screened door on my back porch. Old, ancient, echo-y howling.

Busby stood up on all fours and lifted his left front paw high in the air and pawed at nothing before setting it down again; he teetered to the left, then to the right and plopped down again in the grass.

"There's something seriously funky about your cat," I said.

"No, really, you think so?"

"Not just the dying and living thing," I said. "He's acting really strange."

"Well, Gram says cats *are* strange."

I heard the sound of screeching metal and Rudy's garage door started to rise like a yawning mouth. Busby didn't seem to notice. Rudy and I both turned to see his mother drive their dark blue mini-van up the driveway. She hopped out of the driver's seat and came around to the front of the car, raised her keys in her hand triumphantly and said, "Score!"

Rudy's mother scored once or twice a week. She was what my mother called a Power Shopper. My mom had some coupons in a little black-and-white striped fold-over wallet-type booklet she could put in her purse. Mrs. Albee kept *her* coupons in a two-drawer file cabinet and carried some to the store in a photo-keeper box. She shopped at mega stores with huge discounts and brought home car loads of enormous cans of Chef Boyardee and baked beans.

"See," she said, pointing at Busby, "I told you he wasn't under the refrigerator. Come on boys, help me unload."

This time Mrs. Albee had a car load of paper towels.

"BOGO!" She said.

Only girls knew about BOGO because it was on girlie commercials and I refused to admit to anyone other than Rudy and Mrs. Albee that I understood she hit a buy one, get one free special. There was something *shopping* about it. And I'm allergic to shopping for most things.

"Plus, I had three coupons for fifty cents off!" She was way too happy.

These were eight-packs of paper towels, much lighter than the twelve pack rolls of toilet tissue she brought home a few Saturdays ago when I was unfortunate enough to be at Rudy's. I shouldn't complain. At least she saves the humongous cans for Mr. Albee to unload.

We struggled with a pack of paper towels under each arm and took them into the garage. Three-quarters of the Albee's garage was a maze of tall stacks of groceries that Mrs. Albee had scored. It was organized

8

by some kind of Mrs. Albee logic and a small table in one corner was covered with clip boards–Mrs. Albee shopped for the entire neighborhood. She scored, and they bought from her. One wall of the garage was lined with extra freezers, a working fridge, and the old one that killed Busby just that morning.

"To the back wall with them," she said. She moved a few cases of Diet Coke and Dr. Pepper closer to the door to the house and we stacked our paper towels next to an enormous mound of humongous bags of cat litter.

"Jeez," I whispered. "How much cat litter does Busby need?"

"That reminds me, Alfie," Mrs. Albee said. "You need to bring your red wagon over for some litter. Your mom wants four bags."

I rolled my eyes at Rudy, but he snickered.

After Mrs. Albee went into the house I said, "Why does she always say *my* wagon? It's not my wagon. It's my mom's."

"It used to be your wagon."

"Not anymore. Now it's my mom's."

"Who cares?"

"It makes me sound like I'm four years old and have a red wagon."

"Just bring your red wagon over and take some cat litter."

I can't tell you how awful it would be to have to pull a little red wagon up Sand Hill Road and down Scrub Jay, hauling groceries back and forth, if I were the only one doing it. I imagine I'd feel very silly. But since most of the kids in the neighborhood were stuck doing it, it didn't feel so bad–so long as everyone understood that the wagon was my mom's gardening supply wagon, and not mine. My mom says we should be grateful to have a Power Shopper in the neighbor-hood. And I guess it was pretty neat when Mrs. Albee scored all those boxes of brownie mix.

Chapter Three

That Saturday, Busby bit it again. This time he chewed on an electric cord and blew out some circuits. Rudy's dad was mad and said some things he probably shouldn't have. I was there, so I know. Rudy didn't plan a wake or a funeral this time. He put Busby in his cat bed and went on about his day. We were playing Death Zombies in his room and I kept making excuses to go downstairs into the kitchen so I could take a look to see if Busby was alive again.

Busby had never been a friendly cat; not to me, anyway. And as I stood over him, watching him as if he were sleeping, I had an eerie feeling in my gut. Normally, you can't sneak up on a sleeping cat. Even when they're stretched out on their backs with their front paws stuck up in the air and look like they're in a deep, deep slumber, you come within a few feet of them and they jump up and twitch their ears at you. But I could probably have pet Busby then and he wouldn't do anything...because he was dead. Still, I didn't. I decided to respect the fact that he disliked me.

When I had to leave at five o'clock, unfortunately pulling home a wagon load of "Value Cat" cat litter in something like one-hundred pound bags in my mom's red wagon, Busby was still dead.

"Maybe it'll stick this time," Rudy said following me down the driveway.

"Sure," I grunted. Cat litter is not an easy pull— brownie mix is much lighter. "I mean, electrocution's got to be lethal, right? I mean, truly lethal."

Rudy nodded, but he called me the next day to say that Busby was alive and well and maybe his eyes were just a little bit pink. And maybe he was meowing awfully strange. And his hair was sticking up funny on his back. But his gram said that after all Busby had been through, he had the right to be a bit gnarly. Gnarly is apparently a word his gram uses a lot.

Not that his parents or his gram believed Busby had been dying and living again. They thought he'd had some *scrapes*, as they put it. His gram said Busby was one lucky cat. She said it was a good thing Grant and Brian didn't know how to dig a good hole or Busby would be dead for sure.

"But he was dead, Gram," Rudy said.

"Of course he was," she said with a clever smile.

Does it seem to you that grownups forget things?

Anyway, when my mom came home from work the next afternoon with a colorful cat in a cardboard box, I asked her if I could call her Gnarly and she said okay. My mom likes odd names. We have a hamster named Cow and another cat named Fletch, which reminds me of retching. If either cat looked like somebody vomited on it, it would be Gnarly. She had yellow, white, black, and brown splotches all over her. Mom wanted to call her Calico, but Gnarly was better. What kind of stupid name is Calico, anyway?

"Why'd we get another cat?" my dad asked when he got home.

My mom smiled. "The Diehls are moving to a smaller place. She needed a new home."

"I'm calling her Gnarly," I said and my sister Pearl made a face.

Dad shrugged, just like when we brought Cow home, and sat down in front of the TV to do what my mom called *unwind* while I helped her peel potatoes.

When Busby died the fifth time, I knew for sure something really weird was happening. For one thing, the cats I know don't die that often. I mean, there must be twenty cats in the neighborhood–Natalie has fifteen of them–and so far only one of them has died that I can remember and it was really old and the Ricker's took it to the vet to be put out of its misery. So, even though it was dead, I'm not sure you could count it.

No cats hit by cars. (You saw the occasional carcass on the road on the way to school, but none in the neighborhood.) No electrocutions. No poisonings, and definitely none being squashed flat by large appliances. And absolutely no cat had ever gotten its collar caught on a hook, on the wall below the eighth step of the stairs, and hanged itself. Never.

The hook held strands of holiday lights. Rudy's father is a little crazy. He puts lights up on the inside and outside of the house for every holiday. Valentine 's Day, red. Easter, pink and yellow. Independence Day, of course, red, white, and blue. Halloween, purple and orange. Thanksgiving, yellow and orange. And Christmas, all sorts of colors. Inside, they run upward along the curving wall on the right side of the staircase. It's just inside the front door, so you get to see it a lot.

You might think that's going overboard and lights

ought to be special for Christmas. And then you might think, at least Christmas is more special because they put up a tree; but no, they also have a tree and presents for all the holidays. The tree is fake and stays up all year and they just rotate ornaments. Little stuffed bunnies and large plastic eggs sit on the branches at Easter; witch, pumpkin, and scarecrow ornaments for Halloween. You get the idea.

I sound like I'm making fun, but I like Rudy's house, even if his parents are strange. And even if he's got a zombie cat.

Somehow, apparently, Busby was on the stairs and tried to jump, but changed his mind or stumbled and found himself hanging off the eighth step for dear life, his body dangling high above the ground. And when he slid off, I guess his collar slid onto the hook. His last thought must have been about the twinkling pink and yellow lights left over from Easter. Either that or, *oh no, not again.*

Rudy left him on the hook and called me over to see.

"If I left him there," he said, "and he came alive again, would he die again?"

I nodded. "Probably."

"So, technically," he said, "I could leave him there and see how many times it takes him to really die."

"That would be mean, though. Right?"

Rudy sighed. "I guess."

He walked up to the eighth step, reached down between the stair posts, grabbed Busby by the collar, and pulled him up off the hook, dislodging the string of lights at the same time. He handed the cat to me while he got out a step stool from the kitchen to hang the lights back onto the hook. I took Busby over to the sofa and sat with him on my lap.

"He's really dead," I said. "His tongue's hanging out."

Rudy gave me a *duh* look.

"Well, maybe he wasn't completely dead the other times."

"Not possible. He was totally dead before. Go put him in his bed."

I got up and went into the kitchen, by the window, and laid Busby in his bed and snuck a quick pet. I hoped he wouldn't mind. On my way home I was thinking Busby was a zombie cat. And that meant, naturally, that eventually the zombie cat virus would spread and we'd start turning into zombies and eating one another's brains. And that's when I realized they'd cordon off the neighborhood and trap us in it. And then napalm us, I guess. Of course I laughed it off. There's really no such thing as a zombie virus, right? And if there was, it would be for people, not cats. I mean, who ever heard of zombie cats? Dawn of the Living Zombie Cats? The Walking Zombie Cats? I don't think so.

CHAPTER FOUR

The next week, both my cats died, but only for a few hours. Like I said, in all my twelve years... well, okay the years I can remember, and I'm only almost twelve, I don't recall any cats in the neighborhood dying, except that one that didn't count. Something was really wrong and Rudy agreed.

"What are we going to do?" I said.

"We have to investigate."

"What's to investigate?"

"Plenty."

Rudy dug out a notebook from a big trunk in his bedroom and we sat on his bed, on the Transformers bedspread that I still pretended was too sissy for me, remembering the dates Busby died as best we could. And we added my cats, Gnarly and Fletch, who both drowned in a big barrel of water in the neighbor's yard. Busby again, who fell out of the sixty-foot pine in the lot behind Rudy's. The next day, Gnarly again; she ate something poisonous, we think.

By that time, The Twits were getting together to see our dead pets. We used to call ourselves the The Tweets. Okay, cancel that. Sarah and Natalie used to call us The Tweets. They started it years ago when we were kids, because we live in a little neighborhood called Bird Place. Our streets are named after birds. They tried out all kinds of names: The Beaks, The Hoppers, The Waddlers, The Quackers, The Whistlers. Finally, one of them said Tweets and it stuck. When I told my mom about it, she thought it was a great idea, so I knew it was stupid. But it's just us, not all the kids in the neighborhood. Me and Rudy and Sarah and Natalie. So, what could it hurt, such a name? Grant and Brian found out, of course, and Grant called us The Twits, instead. And I should have seen that coming. But it was too late then, to do anything about it. And for some reason, The Twits stuck a lot harder than The Tweets.

Anyway, then Cow, my sister's hamster, died on his wheel. I put a towel over the cage so Pearl wouldn't have to see him if she got home from the bus stop before I did. I came home from school that day to bury him—it never occurred to me we'd have a zombie hamster problem, too—but I heard the wheel squeaking from all the way out in the hallway.

So, The Twits came over and picked up the dead cats when they had the chance, and Cow, and they shook them; Rudy yelled at them for it. Or they'd cuddle them, because, they'd never held a dead animal before. It was especially nice with Cow because if you tried to hold him when he was alive he wouldn't stop running down your arm and off your hand onto your other hand. Did I mention that Cow died seven times on his wheel in two days?

And that Friday at the bus stop, we heard that other neighborhood animals had started dying. It was the last day of the last full week of school and The Twits gathered at the bus stop to tell Rudy what happened and he put it in the notebook.

One time, in the fourth grade, we had to draw maps of our neighborhoods. Mine looked like a huge piece of layer cake lying on a plate, with four layers; the roads between were chocolate icing. On the left edge, which would be the outside edge of the cake covered in icing, was Sand Hill Road where the Rickers lived. All the houses on Sand Hill back up against the canal, which is really a big ditch, but Mom says canal sounds nicer. The ditch separates our neighborhood from the one behind it where Conrad Duke and Petra Wallace live. We spend long days at the canal with them, fishing and throwing rocks at one another; but nobody goes into the water because of the eleven-foot gator. None of us has seen it; we just know it's there.

Anyway, perpendicular to Sand Hill Road, the four layers of the cake stretched out over to a strip of grass and a really nice sidewalk along Pelican Drive, one of those big roads with a grassy median in the middle. But we can't get to that strip of grass or the sidewalk or Pelican Drive because, so my mom says, the residents here got up a petition to have a brick wall put in–a brick wall too high for us to climb. We're trapped, you see.

Rudy lives on Scrub Jay Road and behind it is the top of the cake where the icing is always really thick because my mom slathers all the leftover on it. That icing is actually empty lots filled with pines and scrub, behind his and all the other houses on Scrub Jay. Behind those woods is a snooty neighborhood with fancy houses where the streets are named after golfers like Hogan, Player, and Nicklaus. The empty acres of land weren't enough to keep the fancy people from having any connection to our little houses, so they put up a fifty-foot tall wood fence to keep us out. I might be exaggerating a little bit.

I live on the next layer, on Sea Gull Road. Then there are Blue Jay and Ibis Roads and that's it. We are sandwiched in here, among other neighborhoods that probably looked like other foods. I thought Kent Zeffert's looked like cauliflower, personally.

The Twits gathered at the stop sign at the end of Sand Hill Road, back packs slung to the ground at our feet. Natalie was shoving a small square piece of French toast in her mouth; her black and gray striped shirt was liberally sprinkled with powdered sugar. Sarah sauntered across Sand Hill and stood, still wearing her backpack, pushing her glasses farther up her nose with her middle finger every three seconds.

"How many times has Busby died?" Natalie said.

I stared at her, because that's what I usually do with Natalie. She's too bright in the mornings. I think it's the way the sun shines off her whitish blond hair. She has really big, clean white teeth, too. She can eat broccoli and none of it ever gets in her teeth. I'm always amazed at that.

"Eight," Rudy said.

"Eight?" I said, pulling myself away from the Natalie light. "We were at six before."

Rudy showed me the notebook. "After falling out of the tree, he suffocated himself in a plastic grocery bag, and yesterday he just showed up dead and all chewed-up looking."

"He's only got one more life left," Sarah said.

"Huh?" Rudy looked at her like she had spoken Japanese.

"Cats have nine lives. Everybody knows that." She

pulled a hand through her long, black hair, absent-mindedly, and shoved her glasses up higher on her nose.

"Don't be stupid," I said. "If they had nine lives, nobody would be surprised when they came back to life. You think all the cats that die and stay dead have just run out of lives?"

"Well, do you have a better explanation?" Sarah tilted her head and raised her eyebrows at me. I really hated it when girls did that.

"No," I said.

"Fine then. Wait and see. One more time and Busby will be totally dead."

"But what about Cow? Nobody ever said hamsters have nine lives."

"Just because nobody ever said it doesn't make it not true."

"Sarah, think about it," Rudy said. "All our pets die one time. They don't have more than one life."

"Maybe," said Natalie, chewing a piece of French toast. She swallowed. "Maybe cats die eight times in the womb, before they're born, you know? And that's why nobody notices them dying eight times."

We all stared at her. I know I was giving her one those 'you're stupid' looks, but everybody else appeared to be actually taking her seriously.

I shook my head. "That's insane."

"Then how do you explain this?" Sarah said.

"It must be a virus or something," Rudy said.

"A zombie virus," I said and they all looked at me with wide eyes. "Sure. It's all because of a zombie virus."

"But, zombies don't keep dying and coming back to life," Natalie said. Everybody nodded at that and she popped her last piece of French toast into her mouth.

"And zombies feed on human flesh," Sarah said.

Natalie was, by this time, picking up the bits of powdered sugar off her shirt with her tongue-licked fingers.

"Human zombies," I said. "These are pets. Maybe the rules for zombies don't work the same in the animal kingdom."

"Hello," Natalie said, slapping her hand on her waist and rolling her head around on her neck, her short blond curls dancing up and down. "We're part of the animal kingdom."

"You know what I mean."

"Well, my mom's taking our cat Fig to the vet this morning," Sarah said. "If he has anything, I'll let you know."

"But Fig hasn't died yet, has he?"

Sarah shook her head and ran her fingers through her hair. "No, and I'd rather he didn't. I don't think my mom could handle it."

"My mom doesn't even believe Busby died. She thinks we overreacted."

"Same here," Natalie said with another shove at the glasses. "My parents think I'm crazy. But I think I know dead when I see it."

"Maybe for the time being," I said, "we should stop talking about this to our parents. They don't understand and I don't want them all freaking out."

Chapter Five

School that day was awful. Somehow word got around that several cats and a hamster in our neighborhood were dying and coming back to life only to die again. But the story grew and grew as the day went on. By lunchtime everybody believed we were locking our cats in outdoor freezers or hanging them from trees. Instead of them coming back to life, kids were saying we were replacing them with cats we stole from surrounding neighborhoods. And when we all got on the bus that afternoon, nobody wanted us sitting next to them. Glaring looks followed us as we walked down the tiny aisle. Somebody hissed, "Cat killers," as we passed.

When we came close to our stop on the corner of Sand Hill and Manatee, I stood up and cleared my throat. "I just want to say that you guys should really think about getting the facts straight before you accuse people of being murderers."

Mrs. Fissnit, the bus driver, looked at me in that

strange mirror she has above her head and shouted, "Sit down, Alfred Whitaker."

Everybody laughed. They always laughed when someone said Alfred.

As we gathered at the bus stop and the bus pulled away, Sarah said, "I think we should stop talking about this whole thing to anybody."

We all nodded in agreement.

"How about we check on our cats and meet out behind my house after dinner," Rudy said.

My mom made spaghetti and I ate a lot, so I thought I was late when I walked down the block to Rudy's. But we waited on the sidewalk in front of his house for Sarah and Natalie. I had a half full box of vanilla wafer cookies for dessert and shoved them in my mouth one after the other; I wanted to get them eaten before Natalie showed up, but I had to share with Rudy–it was only polite. When the cookies were gone and we'd poured out the few crumbs into our palms and licked them up (I've always found it a shame vanilla wafer cookies don't make a lot of crumbs), Rudy was tired of waiting.

"Let's go under the fence and see the puppies," he said.

We walked behind Rudy's house, through the hole in his mom's sweet viburnum hedge, and along the back edges of his neighbors' yards as quietly as we could, so none of them would yell at us to pipe down. We took the path into the woods behind the Saunders' house. You never wanted to sneak behind their house from the front to get to the path, because they were always outside, usually playing basketball in the drive-way and running around in the sprinklers on the front lawn, and the three-year old would want to follow you. There always seemed to be a three-year old Saunders kid trying to follow older kids around.

Anyway, we followed the path into the empty lots and took the left trail to the tall fancy fence that was supposed to keep us out of the ritzy neighborhood, and crawled through the hole where some of the wood planks had been hacked off at the bottom. I should admit that we liked that the snooty people wanted to put up a tall fence. It made our woods eerier and darker and scarier somehow. Maybe it was knowing the only people who should be there were the kids from our neighborhood. Anybody else showing up would have to be a vampire or a chainsaw murderer. We were always on the lookout.

On the other side of the fence, the back yards were bigger, but the houses, strangely enough, were only one story. Still, all of them had pools. In our neighborhood, only Rudy and the Swans had pools and they were pretty small–not that I'm complaining.

Three houses down there were four cocker spaniel puppies behind a chain-link fence. We found them three weeks before on our way to the convenience store on Parr Avenue. I'm pretty sure the hole in the fence was made for that purpose–it's a shorter walk to Wilkie's Stop n Shop for any of us in the slab of cake neighborhood. If there wasn't a hole in the fence, we'd have to walk to the main entrance on Sand Hill, then all the way down Manatee and back up Pelican Drive and onto Parr. It's really not fair when you think about it.

The puppies belonged to Linda Percy; she went to the high school, and Grant had the biggest crush on her–so big he told us if he ever heard about us going over to see the puppies again he'd pound us. So we were all sworn to secrecy. Even Linda, who totally understood when Rudy explained it all to her.

We sat at the chain-link fence around Linda's back

yard and the puppies ran over as soon as they saw us. They licked our fingers and yelped and wagged. Finally, Mrs. Percy saw us; she opened the door and told us we could climb over, so we did. We must have spent a half hour running back and forth being chased by puppies.

When we remembered the girls, and that we were supposed to be having a meeting about the dead cats, we started back, but when we got to the hole in the fence, Mr. Tanturo, who we liked to call Tarantula, started screaming at us about the squirrels again. Mr. Tanturo was positive that squirrels from our neighborhood had invaded his neighborhood and killed off all the good squirrels he had, replacing them with the wrong sorts of squirrels–the kind we had, apparently.

"Get back under the fence where you belong," he yelled. "And take those squirrels with you."

We always tried to pretend to be scared because my mom told us he was a senile old man and yelling at us about the squirrels was probably one of the few joys he had in life. So we screamed and ran and crawled through the hole and then laughed where he couldn't hear us.

Chapter Six

Sarah and Natalie were waiting for us at Rudy's with those looks on their faces–the ones they get whenever we were all supposed to do something and we forget. The whole reason we left in the first place was because we had to wait for them, but you can't argue with Natalie when she's tapping her foot.

"You shouldn't have gone to see the puppies," Sarah said as we all walked behind Rudy's into the woods again, in the other direction. The clearing, where we spent most of our time and made a pact not to reveal its location to any Saunders kid, was behind the Harrison's house.

"Why not?" Rudy said.

"You could give them the zombie virus, of course."

"That's awful," Natalie said. "You think we should tell Linda about it?"

"No!" Rudy and I said it at the same time.

"We agreed not to talk to anybody else about it," I

said. "At least not until we figure out what's going on."

"We should keep an eye on the puppies, though," Natalie said.

"From a distance," Sarah said.

When we trudged into the clearing, Grant and Brian stood at the far side, under the huge oak tree. We all stopped and stared. What were they doing there? They were in high school. They weren't supposed to hang out in the clearing in the woods, anymore. It was our spot now. I was pretty sure there was a rule that said when one of your friends can drive and gets a car, you aren't allowed to climb trees and hang out in the woods, or play in the ditch behind the Ricker's, or walk to the convenience store. Older kids had a code, didn't they?

The others got over their shock easily enough and went on, but not me. My heart pattered off beat at the sight of Alien Watley. It wasn't like I'd never been near him before. He was usually over at Rudy's with Grant. But he always only gave me the big, bug-eye stare and frowned like he wanted to punch me. I had never, ever, ever in my life 'hung out' with Brian Watley. And standing under the oak in the woods behind the Harrison's was hanging out. I had to start walking or I'd be standing at the end of the path all by myself like a dork, so I trudged on, trying not to look at The Alien.

When we were kids, Grant helped us nail thick wood slats into the oak, so we could climb it. We started to build a tree house, but never made it past some ropes tied to branches. The limbs were so large and thick we decided we didn't really need any floors or walls. We could spend days up in that tree if we had to. But now it seemed to cast an eerie shadow in the woods with Alien Watley standing next to the enormous trunk, shaded by low hanging branches.

The older kids turned to look at us as we approached. I managed to make my feet move toward them, and stand with them, feeling odd and out of place. Something is not quite right about older kids, and it's the very something that makes them look older. They don't have to do anything, just stand there... looking older. Is it the slouch? Or the way their shirts hang off their lanky frames?

Whatever it was, I guess we should have been glad they weren't vampires. I had to admit to myself that Alien Watley wasn't quite as scary as a vampire. Sarah was big on vampires and said she laid out a circle of garlic salt on the ground around the tree to keep them out so we'd always have a place of shelter if they attacked. Older kids weren't as much fun as vampires would be. But they had their moments.

Natalie and Sarah started giggling and nudging each other almost right away and I knew it was because of Grant. They said he looked like some singer or actor guy, I don't know which one. They said he was a heart battery or something stupid like that. He was just a kid. A kid with a lot of muscles and light brown hair sticking up at odd angles on his head. But, hey, if that's what girls like.

"I forgot." I looked at Sarah. "What happened at the vet with Fig?"

She lifted his shoulders and put her palms in the air. "Beats me. My mom's not home from work, yet."

"We're going to turn into zombies," Grant said.

Chapter Seven

I was stunned by his remark. My mouth fell open and I shivered as I imagined Grant lumbering awkwardly toward me, his actor-guy hair now wiry and stiff and the dead skin flaking off his heart-battery face. Natalie and Sarah wouldn't be giggling then, would they?

"Why would you think that?" Rudy said, completely unaffected by the zombie possibilities.

"You said the cats are zombies and if we're infected..."

"Wouldn't we be zombies by now? Or at least dying and living again?" I said, the images in my head getting worse. But, what I said made perfect sense to me. I looked at Grant and even though he wasn't making any noise, he was laughing at me.

"I agree," Rudy said. "Whatever is happening, it has to do with a lot of dying. So, if anybody dies, we need to spread the word."

"I don't want to die," Sarah said.

"Spread the word?" I said. "We won't have to spread the word. Everyone will know."

"Don't freak out," Rudy said. "We'd probably already be dying if we were going to. I mean, Busby's died a gazillion times already and I haven't died once."

"That's true," Grant said and it was nice of him to take us seriously.

"Let's just keep logging the info, like we have been. And let's meet up here every night and see what's new," Rudy said.

"I don't know," Brian Watley spoke up. Like I said, I didn't spend much time in the Alien's presence, but when I did, he never said anything. Brian had these black-rimmed glasses with super thick lenses that made his eyes look huge; and his hair was really long, way past his shoulders. The other older kids called him a surf geek; but I didn't see it. When he looked at you really hard with his humongous magnified eyes, you got the feeling he was secretly an alien—the kind of alien who could mash you up and spread you on toast and eat you. I don't think I ever called Brian Watley an alien to anyone but Rudy. I was way too chicken I'd be found out and he'd eat me.

"I don't think we should meet at night. In the dark," he said.

"Wh-wh-what'd you mean?" I said. The last time I said something to Brian Watley it came out the same way. But nobody laughed this time.

"If the cats do become zombies after their ninth life, as Sarah suggests..." he said.

"Where'd you hear about that?" Natalie said.

I wanted to say, yeah, yeah, where'd you hear about that, but honestly, I was still afraid the Alien might eat me.

"I told Grant about it," Rudy said.

"We weren't supposed to tell," Sarah said.

"It's okay. They can help," Rudy said.

But did we want their help? That's what I wanted to know.

"I said they'd die for good after their eighth life," Sarah said.

Brian looked at her, skeptical. "I'm thinking they'll become more violent after their ninth death."

"How come?" Rudy said.

"I watch a lot of zombie movies," Brian said. "Zombies are slow, and decaying and all, but they're strong and definitely violent. Zombies like to eat people's brains. But they'll eat their other insides, too."

"You think a few little cats are going to eat our brains?" Grant said with a laugh.

I laughed too, even though I was still afraid of Brian. But the rest of The Twits looked around, terrified–not of Brian the Alien, standing with us in the shade of the oak tree talking to us like we were equals, but of having our brains eaten out of our skulls, which I had to admit was probably more of a concern.

Brian nodded slowly. "They'll come after us, relentlessly, until we're too exhausted to run from them anymore. And they'll claw at our bodies, and eat our brains."

"But how can we stop them?" Sarah asked shoving her glasses onto her nose several times, like it was a comfort.

"We'll have to hack off their little heads and toss their little cat bodies into a pile and set them all on fire."

Everybody stared at Brian, our eyes growing wide in the dim light, trying to take in as much as we could.

Finally, I broke the spell. "Aw, come on," I said. "They're cats."

"Zombie cats," Natalie said sarcastically. "You think you can just hiss at them and make them run. They're not drinking from the toilet here, you know. This is serious."

"We don't know that, yet. Let's not jump to conclusions."

"All right, all right. Let's continue to meet in the mornings at the bus stop. In daylight. Is that okay?" Rudy said.

"There are only three days left of school," Natalie said.

"We can meet out here in the summer," Rudy said. "In the morning."

The Twits nodded, but I was horrified. I did not want to spend my summer trying to stop a zombie cat attack. I wanted to swim at my Gram's and go to the beach at her condo and go to Disney World. But they all seemed to settle in, like this was a long haul zombie project. The older kids were smiling at us in that way my mom talks about–patronizing is the word she used, I think, like they're patting us on the heads.

"You keep us posted, little twits," Grant said.

Sarah sighed. "It's birds. We're The Tweets."

Grant rolled his eyes and nudged Brian, but The Alien wouldn't laugh with him.

"You do get that they're going for the whole bird thing, right?" Brian said to him.

"Yeah," Grant said, still chuckling. "Stupid, isn't it."

"It's because of our streets," Sarah said. "We live on streets named after birds."

Grant stopped laughing and looked quickly around at the group.

Sarah said, "Scrub Jay, Sea Gull, Ibis, Blue Jay. They're birds."

Sarah has this sarcastic, snotty way of talking and she lifts her nose up while she does it and makes you feel really small.

"Seriously, dude," Brian said. "You didn't get their name?"

Grant put his hands on his hips and smiled. "I did not put it together. No. But you have to admit, twits is funnier."

Grant walked out from under the oak and headed down the path back to Rudy's house. I turned to look at Brian Watley. In the fading daylight his large eyes seemed to glow through his lenses.

"You guys really think something's going on here?" I asked.

"Of course we do," Brian said.

"I just didn't think you would," I said. "Our parents don't believe us. Why would you?"

The darkness seemed to come out of nowhere and an owl hooted in the distance.

"Well, I'm getting out of here," Sarah said.

Natalie went with her, but Brian the Alien stayed for a minute and looked at me and Rudy. I swallowed hard, for some reason expecting him to pick me up and toss me into the tree.

"Keep us posted," he said.

"I will," Rudy said.

Brian lived across the street from Rudy. Rudy says Grant remembers him before he got glasses and he wasn't nearly as scary, maybe because he ran into things a lot back then.

Once everyone had left, I turned to Rudy. "You don't really think they're going to try to eat our brains, do you?"

He shrugged. "That's what zombies do, isn't it?"

"But zombies are undead people and they try to eat

people brains. Maybe the cats will only try to eat cat brains."

"At the rate the virus is spreading, there won't be any living cats left for them to eat."

It was dark now and I heard a twig snap somewhere south, toward the snooty privacy fence. I shivered.

Chapter Eight

Sometime in the night, I woke up with something clawing at my hair; it was Gnarly, trying to chew on my brains. I screamed and sat up, tossing the cat off me. My mom and dad came into my room and turned on the light.

"Gnarly was going to eat my brains," I said.

"I tried to find her," my mother said picking Gnarly up, "and put her out when I came home this evening. She must have been hiding. I'm sorry."

"You mean she really was trying to eat his brains?" Dad said, but you could tell he was joking.

"Don't be silly. She eats kibble," Mom said.

"She was trying to eat my brains, I tell you."

"I'll put her out now."

"Aren't you going to look at my head? Is there a hole? Did she get any brains out?"

My dad said, "Don't be a goof. Do you know how thick your skull is? That measly cat couldn't crack it. Go on back to sleep."

But I couldn't go back to sleep. I could still feel Gnarly's sharp little teeth pulling at my hair. My cat was a zombie. Was I going to have to cut her head off and burn her corpse? I didn't think I could do that. It would take a really sick sort of person to be able to do such an awful thing–somebody like Alien Watley.

The next morning was Saturday but I couldn't sleep past seven. What sort of world do we live in when a kid can't stay asleep on a Saturday morning? Mom was in the kitchen singing one of those songs from when she was a kid; it reminded me of Busby's meow.

"Good morning," she trilled. "Cereal?"

I moaned and rubbed my eyes. After a few bites of Cheerios I started to feel awake.

"Mom," I said. "If Gnarly and Fletch got really sick, what would we do?"

She sat down across from me and took a slurp of her yogurt. She glanced at her open magazine and then looked at me. "What do you mean by sick?"

"I mean, with a contagious disease."

"We'd take them to the vet and see if we could have them cured."

"What if we couldn't? What if what they had was really bad and there was no cure?"

"Well, then, I'm afraid we'd have to have them euthanized."

"Euthanized? What's that?"

"Put to sleep."

"Like the Ricker's cat?"

"Exactly. Fluffy was very old and in a lot of pain. She couldn't keep food down, anymore. It was best to let her die peacefully."

"What if all the cats in the neighborhood caught this disease?"

"That would be awful."

"They'd kill all of them?"

"If they had to. Does this have anything to do with last night?"

"What about last night?"

"You said Gnarly was trying to eat your brains. Bad dream?"

"Yeah, I guess."

"Well, don't let it bother you. As far as I know the cats in the neighborhood are healthy."

"Are there any diseases, though, that can't be cured?"

"Sure, there's rabies, right? And maybe distemper. And there's a feline virus that is very contagious and I don't think there's a cure for it. I don't remember what it's called." She turned to her magazine carelessly. "FUS, maybe? No, no, that's the one where they can't pee and their bladder swells up."

"Mom! *Ew.*"

"But we all take our cats to the vet and have them tested and they get their shots. So, you shouldn't worry."

I mumbled under my breath, "Me, worry?"

"Only three more days until your graduation."

"I'm not wearing a dress."

"It's called a gown, and you don't have to. But you do have to wear a nice button-up shirt and a tie."

"Aw. Can't I just skip it?"

"Nope."

That was that, I guess. At least I didn't have to wear a dress.

"Oh, by the way," she said without looking up from her magazine. "I need you to take your wagon over to Rudy's and pick up more of that cat food. I'll get you some money to pay Mrs. Albee."

"It's your wagon."

"You can take Pearl's wagon, if you'd rather."

I sputtered and a soggy Cheerio flew out of my mouth. "You want me to pull a pink wagon down to Rudy's?"

She smiled and looked up at me. "I don't mind if you take yours. I don't need it today."

One of these days I'm going to bury that wagon in the back yard.

Chapter Nine

After trudging with my mom's wagon to Rudy's and hauling back one of those huge bags of Power Shopping cat food, I met The Twits that morning in the empty lot. Grant was standing against the oak when we arrived. You could almost feel the air get lighter around Sarah and Natalie. I had to admit, Grant did look like he was modeling jeans or something, like in one of those commercials. You know those TV ads where older kids stand funny and say things that don't make a lot of sense? One of those.

"Did you find out about the vet, yet?" I asked Sarah.

"Perfect health," she said with a frown, mid-chew on a boiled egg. "But he died."

"What happened?" Natalie asked.

"Hit by a car. I swear he ran right out in front of it. It was Mr. Phelps driving and he stopped and asked me if he was okay. I said he was fine, but I don't think he believed me. I scraped Fig off the road and wrapped him in a towel and brought him home."

"And?" Rudy said.

"He woke up again. Just like your cats. Mr. Phelps came over later and asked if he was dead."

"What did you do?" I asked with a warning look.

"I told him he wasn't. *Duh.* I told him he was only knocked out. Don't worry, my parents don't know anything."

"What are we going to do?" Rudy said.

"I'll tell you what we're not going to do," I said. "We're not going to tell anybody about it."

"We already decided that, right?" Rudy said.

"Right. And now we're going to make a pact."

"What's the big deal?" Brian said, coming from the path into the clearing.

"If people find out about this virus, they'll euthanize our cats," I said.

"You mean, put them to sleep?" Natalie said.

"Yeah, except they don't sleep, right? They die."

Grant laughed loudly and we all turned to him where he stood leaning against the oak. "If they euthanize them," he said. "Wouldn't they just come back to life again?"

We all looked at one another, back and forth, our brows knit together in confusion.

"I guess I hadn't thought of that," I said. "But then, if they come back to life, they'll know for sure something is going on and then NASA or the FBI will come over here and quarantine our neighborhood."

"Cool," Grant said.

"It's not cool," I said. "I don't want to be stuck here. I want to go to the beach this summer and to Disney World. Don't you?"

Grant shrugged and looked at Brian. I could tell they were laughing at me.

"It wouldn't be NASA," Grant said. "Or the FBI. It would probably be *Animal Cops*."

"Houston or Detroit?" Brian said.

"Miami. We're in Florida. Why would they send Houston?" Grant said.

"Don't they have *Animal Cops* here in Palm Gardens?" Natalie said.

"No," Brian said. "Only the big cities can afford *Animal Cops*."

"Yeah, I think you're right," Sarah said. "They'd send Miami."

"What are you guys talking about?" I felt a huge surge of fear and power flowing through me and heard my voice echoing all around the empty lot. "Who cares who they send? We're going to be quarantined. They'll kill and burn all the cats and then wait to see if we catch whatever horrible virus it is floating around. Quarantined."

Grant and Brian looked at me, dully, like they didn't care.

"Cool," Grant said.

I turned to Rudy. "Why did we invite them, anyway?"

"Nobody invited us," Brian said.

"Well, why don't you go home, then?"

"We need them," Natalie said, pulling a plastic sandwich bag filled with boiled eggs out of her pants pocket.

"Do not," I said.

"Yeah, we do," Sarah said. "They're older."

"How are we going to do it?" Rudy said.

"Do what?" Sarah asked.

"Cut off their heads."

"*Whoa, whoa*! Nobody's cutting off my cats' heads," I said.

"He's right," Brian said. "We're not at that point, yet. Maybe we can find another way."

"Like what?" Grant said.

"What causes viruses?" Sarah said.

"The plague!" Natalie said with a wide smile.

"Yeah, the plague," I said, thinking she'd lost her mind. "What about it?"

"The plague was spread by fleas on rats, right?"

"Giant gerbils," Brian said.

"What?" Sarah said.

I think we all agreed with her.

"They've recently postulated that it wasn't the black rats, after all; the plague was likely carried to Europe on giant Asian gerbils."

"I...well, we..." I sputtered. But Brian wasn't paying any attention to us, anymore. He was thinking. He turned his magnified eyes to each of us and I thought his glasses ought to have a warning on them—same as the one on the side-view mirrors on my mom's car: eyes in glasses could seriously be just as enormous as they appear!

"It was still the fleas, though, wasn't it?" Natalie muttered.

"Fleas," Brian mused. "That's a possibility. But the plague wasn't a virus. It was a bacterial infection."

"What difference does that make?" Rudy said.

"Quite a lot, actually."

"But just because we're calling it a zombie virus, doesn't mean it *is* a virus."

"If we don't know what it is, we probably shouldn't be trying to treat it," Brian said.

"So, we need to de-flea the cats," Grant said with a smile.

Brian shrugged.

"I'm not sure my cats have fleas," I said.

"They may have gotten the virus from another cat that was infected," Grant said. "Even so, if we treat them for fleas, it could have some effect on the virus."

Brian rolled his eyes. "I don't think flea prevention will have any effect on a virus or a bacterial infection."

"It's worth a try, isn't it?" Sarah said.

"Does everyone have flea stuff at home?" Natalie looked around at us.

We all shook our heads.

"Nobody treats their cats for fleas?"

"Well," Sarah said, "summer just started and that's when the fleas get bad."

"We can't wait for our parents to get some. We need some now. A lot."

"One dose for each cat?" Grant said.

"More," Brian said. "If we're talking zombie-virus-infected cats, we might need several doses–if it even works at all."

"Where are we going to get that much fleas stuff?" Natalie said.

Everybody turned in unison to look at Rudy and Grant.

Chapter Ten

Rudy and I were selected for the mission. Our goal? Slink our way through the Power Shopping maze in Rudy's garage in search of three-inch by five-inch packets of flea control medication for cats. My mom used to say something about a needle and a hay stack and it was echoing in my head as we stood looking at the ceiling-high columns of groceries, packed neatly in the garage.

"On the other hand," Rudy whispered, "it's bulk shopping, right? So she'd have bought a case or two."

"How big are those?"

Rudy put his hands up in front of him and gestured something like the size of a shoe box. I turned back to the stacks and shook my head sadly. This could take days.

"And she keeps the cat stuff all together in the back."

Now there was hope. We made our way into the maze and to the back of the garage where the enormous bags of cat litter and kibble were piled neatly against the wall. Quietly, we moved plastic boxes filled with deodorants and tooth brushes, cases of canned soup, and bags of potato chips on cardboard pallets wrapped in plastic wrap.

"There's nothing here for cats but food and litter," I said.

"Wait," Rudy whispered. "Look back there."

To my right, on the other side of the garage door leading into the house, there was a stack of shoe boxes marked, "medicines."

"What are these?" I asked, lifting a set of crutches from where three sets leaned against the wall.

"Crutches," Rudy said.

"*Duh*. I know they're crutches. Why does your mom have three sets?"

"They must have been really cheap," he said.

We took boxes off the stack and looked through them for cat medications. When we heard his mother calling from inside the house, we froze and looked at each other, ready to toss the boxes back on the heap and run. But her voice faded off into another part of the house and we began rummaging again.

"Bingo," Rudy said. He'd pulled a large box from behind two stacks. It was a case of flea control.

His mom's voice echoed in the house again, coming closer to the door.

"Hurry," I said, pushing Rudy toward the path between stacks. We worked our way through the maze and darted out of the garage just as we heard the door open and his mother saying, "Nothing to eat? There's plenty to eat. Look around."

We showed up in the clearing by the oak in triumph.

"All right," Grant said. "Now what?"

"Now we put this stuff on every cat in the neighborhood and see what happens," Brian said.

"We need to be organized about it," Rudy said picking his notebook off the ground and sitting down with it. "I need to know who is treating which cats."

We took our packets of flea control and set out on our quests. I just had to do my two cats. Rudy had to do Busby and then help Sarah with hers. Natalie would do her three. Grant and Brian were going to prowl the neighborhood treating the unsuspecting neighbors' cats.

I shoved my two capsules of flea medication into my pants pocket and went into my house to search for Gnarly and Fletch. They like the outdoors well enough, but spend most of their days in the family room lying in the rays of sun that traveled slowly across the carpet, glistening through the blinds. But they weren't there.

"What are you doing?" my mom asked, calling out from the back porch through the opened sliding door.

"I'm looking for the cats."

"They're out here with us."

I walked across the room and peered into the porch. My parents were sitting at the wrought iron table playing Scrabble. Gnarly and Fletch were curled up on one of the padded chairs, sleeping. I stared at them, trying to figure out how to get them away from my parents.

"Well, there they are," Mom said.

I walked over, picked up Fletch, and carried him toward the door.

"Where are you going?" she asked.

"Rudy wants to see him."

I walked back through the house and out the front door. Now what? I couldn't actually take him to Rudy's. I'd have to do it right there on the front porch.

I put Fletch down and took one of the vials out of my pocket. Fletch went straight to the front door, waiting for me to reopen it.

"In a second," I whispered and sat down, pulling him onto my lap. "Okay, so how's this work?"

Fletch was great. He purred at me while I uncapped the vial, pulled at the hair on his neck and squirted the stuff on. He didn't much care for the sensation and hopped off my lap, but he only went to the door again. I opened it, feeling very pleased with myself and went out to get Gnarly.

"Back already?" my mom said. She looked up from her rack of letter tiles curiously.

"Yeah," I said. "Rudy's right out front."

She shook her head and my father looked up at me from over the rims of his reading glasses. As he laid tiles out on the board, he said, "Why doesn't Rudy come out here and see the cats?"

Good question. I stood with my mouth open for a second or two and then the oddest thing came out of my mouth. "He's eating an ice cream sundae," I said. "It's all over him."

Now this wasn't altogether unheard of. In fact, last summer Rudy had done that very thing and walked into our house. When those two little drips of ice cream and hot fudge landed on my mom's foyer tiles it was like sending out a thunderous mopping signal directly to her brain, because she was right there in a flash, turning Rudy around and sending him back outside. I lifted my chin triumphantly. That was a great excuse.

My mom was nodding knowingly, probably re-membering her foyer tiles, so I picked up Gnarly. She wasn't as happy as Fletch to leave her spot on the seat cushion, but I held tight.

"Why does Rudy want to see the cats?"

50

"Uh," I said. I turned and walked quickly out of the room. "To see if they like ice cream."

I cringed. What if my mom didn't want the cats to eat ice cream? I hurried through the house, clinging hard to Gnarly, and took her out onto the front porch. I waited a minute or two, struggling to keep Gnarly in my arms, but mom didn't show up. I grabbed the other vial from my pocket and sat down. The cat squirmed. I stuck her between my legs and tried to hold the vial and twist off the cap, but Gnarly started to hop away. I grabbed at her with my elbows and squeezed my knees on either side of her and popped the lid off. I had to let go with my elbows to push the hair from her neck and just as I got the tip of the vial to her skin she jerked out from between my knees and dashed across the lawn into the street.

Chapter Eleven

Gnarly," I called. I fell over the porch step trying to follow her, rolled over onto the grass and got up to run. She was already across the street under Mrs. Walford's little red car. I lay down on the Walford's driveway and scooted under the car a little bit.

"Come on Gnarly," I said, reaching my hand out to her.

She let me pet her, so I grabbed at her front leg and yanked. She didn't care much for that and nipped at my knuckles.

"Ow," I yelled and let her go.

She edged over a little farther, out of reach, so I scooted out and went around to the other side. I flattened myself out on the ground again and looked under the car, but Gnarly was gone.

"Aw, man," I said.

"Can I help you?"

Mrs. Walford was standing outside her garage door,

wearing a yellow bathing suit, dark sunglasses, and curlers in her hair.

"My cat was under your car," I said.

She chomped up and down on some gum and smiled at me.

"That him over there?" She pointed across the street at the Welch's.

I darted back to the other side of Sea Gull to the house next to mine, but Gnarly took off as soon as I hit the Welch's sidewalk. She ran down Sea Gull, through everybody's yards and only stopped when she got to Tim Krenshaw's house. I caught up with her, huffing and puffing, as she jumped up onto the lid of their trash can, onto the low wall jutting out from the side of their house, and down into their side yard.

"Gnarly," I hissed. "Come back here."

Reluctantly, I followed her toward their fence. I leaped for her as she jumped onto the chain-link gate, and fell face first into it as Gnarly loped across their back yard.

I walked around the Krenshaw's fence and Gnarly didn't seem the least bit concerned as she climbed over it, and ran across the Overland's side yard, heading for Blue Jay Road. She found Natalie's house and their big gardenia bushes out front, just as I got to her driveway.

Natalie came out her front door, scratches on her forearms and left cheek, stuffing a sandwich into her mouth.

"Hey, Alfie," she said casually. "What's up?"

"What happened to you?"

She smiled wide, chewing her sandwich. "Cat."

I nodded and smirked. "Me too. Mine's in your gardenias."

We got on all fours in her driveway where it ran along the front of her house next to the bushes and crawled around looking for Gnarly. She'd tucked herself in the far corner, under the first bush by Natalie's front door. She looked content. But I was determined.

"You don't want to crawl under there," Natalie said.

"I have to. I'm going to squirt this stuff on her neck if it's the last thing I do."

"It might be," Natalie said. She laughed, very pleased with herself.

I pushed my way on my belly, under the thick, waxy green bush, cooing softly to the cat as I inched closer; she looked at me like I was turning away from all that was human. Prickly branches drew themselves sharply across the skin on my arms and face and I knew I was going to come out of it looking worse than Natalie. Gnarly let me grab her. I pulled her under me to hold her down, reached behind me, pulled the darn vial out of my pants pocket and squirted what was left of it on Gnarly's neck. The rest had leaked into my jeans.

"That's just going to have to do," I told Gnarly.

She repaid me by pushing her back claws against my face as she escaped from under me.

"Here I am," I yelled, "at most, curing you of the zombie virus, and at least preventing you from getting fleas, and this is how you repay me?" I don't think the cat understood.

"You want me to pull you out by the feet?" Natalie said.

"*Nah.*"

I pushed backward and wiggled my way out from under the bush. Natalie smiled broadly at me and together we walked across Blue Jay to Sarah's house.

"Nat," I said, a bit out of breath. "I'm not sure I

want to help Sarah."

She laughed and shoved more sandwich in her mouth.

Sarah had two cats left of her seven. When I said she had fifteen, I just meant it seemed like it. Everywhere you went in Sarah's house, you met up with a cat.

"I really appreciate this," Mrs. Johnston called from the kitchen, banging pots and pans around as she emptied the dishwasher. "It's flea season already. Tell Rudy's mom I'll pay her for the flea stuff as soon as I get over there again."

"No problem," I said, passing through the living room and out onto Sarah's back porch. "She doesn't even know we're doing it."

"Really?" She stopped, holding a pan as if she was going to hit someone with it.

"I don't think she'll mind," I said. "It's a good deed, you know?"

She nodded. "Sure, I guess."

Once out on the porch, I saw Rudy was already there.

"I got most of them done," Sarah said. "But I've had some trouble with the others."

Rudy rolled his eyes and held up his arm to show a long red scratch from his elbow to his wrist. Natalie and I held up our arms, too.

"Well, I don't know if scratching is the problem with the last two," Sarah said.

"What's the problem then?"

"Getting to them."

"Where are they?"

Rudy looked at me with a funny smile and then looked up.

"On the roof," Sarah said.

Natalie let out a big laugh and nearly choked on the last bite of her sandwich. "I'm not climbing onto the roof," she said.

"How'd the cats get up there?"

"They climbed the tulip tree," Sarah said, pointing to the tree next to the house.

"Great," I said.

"I'm sure they'll come down later," Sarah said.

"We need to make sure it gets done now," I said. "Come on Rudy, let's go up there. We'll scare them down and you two catch them."

"Okay, but be quiet. I don't think my mom would want you on the roof."

"I don't want to be on the roof."

Rudy and I climbed the tulip tree and hoisted ourselves onto the sloping roof. The tiles, baking in the midday sun, burned our hands. We walked up as quietly as we could and saw the cats just over the ridge on the front side of the house.

"We need to get around them and scare them back to the tulip tree," I said.

We each took a side and approached them. They let us get within a few feet of them before they darted over toward the left. We ran to the left and tried to herd them back to the right and over the ridge but they ran all the way over to the right side of the house.

"We can corner them," I said, "and keep them from going left again."

We walked toward them, on their left side, with our arms outstretched thinking that would make us look bigger and scarier. They darted to the ridge and over to the back side, but went left again instead of hitting the tulip tree. Like that, we chased Sarah's cats around and around her roof until her mother came out back and screamed at us.

"Get off the roof! What do you think you're doing up there? I've never heard such pounding in all my life. If you fall and break your necks what am I supposed to tell your parents?"

You know how adults talk. We climbed back down only to find Sarah and Natalie holding onto the cats for dear life, waiting for her mother to stop screaming and go back inside. I was huffing and puffing by that time and sweat ran down the front and back of my t-shirt and trickled out of my hair.

"That's all the cats we were supposed to do," Rudy said, breathing in hard gasps.

I nodded. "Let's go."

We walked through the neighbors' yards, across Sea Gull and Scrub Jay to Rudy's and out back into the woods where we waited for Brian and Grant to show up.

"Now what?" I said when we all stood around looking at one another.

"Now we wait, I guess," Brian said.

"What are we waiting for, exactly?"

"For them to die."

Chapter Twelve

Waiting wasn't as hard as I thought it would be. For one thing, we had three short days left of school, and each afternoon I had to go to my mom's office to spend the rest of the day with her. It was one thing, she said, to wait two hours alone at home for her to finish work like I usually do. But it was a whole other thing to wait five and a half. Imagine that. Five and a half hours at home, alone. Well, Pearl was always there and I had to watch her or make sure she got over to her friend Katy's house. But without parents, it would be like living all by yourself. You could open the refrigerator any time you wanted and eat whatever you wanted and watch television or play whatever games you wanted.

I got to do that for two hours every day after school before Mom got home from work, except I had to spend twenty minutes walking Pearl over to the far end of Scrub Jay to Katy's most days. And I had to make Pearl a snack, too. And then it seemed like there was only a little bit of time left before Mom would show up so I couldn't get too involved in anything really fun. But no. It was out of the question, apparently, for me to ride the bus home.

Until the third day. Graduation Day. Rudy and I had to wear nice shirts and ties to school that morning. I thought the other kids on the bus would laugh at us, but instead, we seemed to get more respect. I respected them for that respect and vowed to treat them much nicer when they showed up at Sandy Palms Junior High in a year. Some of them I might not see again until I went to Palm Gardens High School. But I probably wouldn't remember them so I didn't make any nice vows about that.

At noon, all of the sixth graders were called into the lunch room where the tables had been cleared away. We were seated in chairs on the stage that hardly ever gets used and is usually hidden by a thick, black velvet curtain. I was in the very back row. But I wouldn't be last. After me were Bobby Wright, the three Youngs–Pam, Cyndi, and Paul–and Kent Zeffert.

All of our parents showed up, well most of them, I guess, and sat in the first rows of folding chairs down on the floor. Some of the other kids were allowed to sit up front with them–brothers and sisters and some best friends. The rest of the room was filled with the entire school.

Speeches were endured and the chorus class sang too many songs and then our names were called and we got to shake the principal's hand and get a certificate. It was almost like we were really graduating and not just moving on to another school for more of the same, only harder.

And after, we all got to climb or jump down from the stage–we were either allowed to do it, or no one saw us in time to yell at us–and find our parents. My mom and dad were smiling really big and Pearl gave me a hug.

"Well," my mom said. "I think, now that you've graduated the sixth grade, you're ready to be at home alone for longer than a couple of hours."

"You mean I can take the bus?"

She nodded. "But you have to make sure Pearl gets to Katy's house, as usual, okay? And Mrs. Ratchet across the street said she'd check in on you."

"No problem."

And it really was no problem. I didn't think about the cats at all. On the bus ride home all I could do was brag to Rudy that I would have my whole house to myself for five hours. Five hours. I could take off my clothes and run around naked if I wanted to. The girls on the bus giggled at that. But it was true. Not that I would do that, but I could have if I'd wanted to. Instead, I got Pearl a snack and walked her over to Katy's house so she could stay with her and her mom. And then I went to Rudy's.

I knew I should go home and revel in the alone time, but I was there on Scrub Jay, anyway. And that's when I started thinking about the cats again. I was thinking about the scratches most of us had on our arms. I don't know why it hadn't occurred to me before. But what if the zombie virus was spread through the scratches?

Rudy was sitting out on his front porch on a rocker eating a ham sandwich.

"Has Busby gotten any better?" I didn't waste any time with hello.

"Yeah," Rudy said. He stood and brushed the crumbs off his shirt. "His eyes don't seem pink at all, anymore, and his fur is looking smoother. Maybe it worked."

"Maybe. Or maybe whatever they had is getting better."

"Maybe we imagined the whole thing. Maybe they weren't really as dead as we thought."

"I guess," I said. And at that moment I thought it could be true. The sun was bright and hot on our faces and the whole summer was ahead of us. Maybe it was just the anxiety of the end of school and graduation that made us nervous. But then, it would have had to infect the others as well. But I've heard of that kind of thing happening. One or two people get hysterical and the next thing you know an entire neighborhood is insane. It could have happened. The whole episode could have ended, whatever it was.

But it wasn't over.

Chapter Thirteen

Rudy walked with me over to Mrs. Ratchet's house, so I could check in with her and let her know I wasn't at home when she tried to check in on me. Mrs. Ratchet lived alone across the street from me. My mom was always going over to check on her and take in her mail. It was my job to carry her trash cans down to the curb and back on trash days. She was a really nice lady with gray hair who wore her pajamas and pink slippers outside while she watered her yard with a hose.

I knocked on her door but she didn't answer. I knocked again and rang the bell. Finally she opened the door and peered out at us with red-rimmed eyes and a tissue clutched in her hand.

"Oh," she said, "Alfie. Is everything all right? I was supposed to check on you today."

"Are you all right?" I said.

"Oh, dear," she said, like old ladies do. "No, I'm afraid my Donald is dead."

I looked at Rudy and he looked back at me wide-eyed.

"Are you sure he's dead?" I said.

"I can't get him to wake up," she said.

"Can we take a look?" Rudy said.

Mrs. Ratchet nodded her gray head and let us in her house. It was stuffy and smelled like moth balls and bacon. And it was cluttered in a neat, organized way. Every shelf and surface had stuff on it. My mom called it knickknacks–but it was really just weird stuff. There were a lot of little cat figures. Mom said I used to play with them when I was little, even though they're breakable. And Mrs. Ratchet sometimes told me I could have them when she died. But you know, you shouldn't talk about old people dying. At least, I'd rather not. Because, well, it's really going to happen and I'd rather not think about Mrs. Ratchet dead. Anyway, I don't think it's polite to accept things you're going to get when somebody dies. That's like saying they really are going to die...even though they are. You know what I mean.

She led us to the back of the house where Donald was lying curled up in his cat bed tucked up against the bar and next to the sliding glass door. Rudy and I knelt beside him and touched him. We exchanged knowing looks.

"He's fine," I said. "He'll be up and about in no time."

"Oh, dear me," she began crying. "Thank you. I thought I'd lost him."

"Well, he's old, Mrs. Ratchet," Rudy said. "He's probably going to go, sometime."

She smiled at him through her tears and nodded. "I was hoping I would die first," she said.

There she went, talking about dying again. While I

had to admit she looked really, really old, I doubted Donald could outlive her, even if he wasn't a zombie now. Donald was the oldest cat I knew. He sat old and meowed old and walked old, all hunched over and everything. And he was grouchy, just like I remember Mr. Ratchet being before he, you know...died.

After we said good-bye to Mrs. Ratchet, we headed over to Rudy's again to find Grant. He and Brian the Alien were sitting around the kitchen table with the Risk game out. I shuddered a little bit, seeing Brian, mostly because he looked up at me and squinted his big eyes from behind his thick lenses, like he was angry at me and just waiting for a chance to pound me into the floor. It's a shame, really, when you think about it. But if you look like you're going to hit people, I expect people are going to imagine you doing it.

"Did you guys do Mrs. Ratchet's cat?" I asked.

"I did," Grant said, rolling the dice.

"Well, he's dead."

They looked at each other.

"Dead dead? Or zombie dead?"

"Um, well," I said.

"We told Mrs. Ratchet he'd be all right," Rudy said.

"But you don't know that. What if the flea stuff worked and Donald's just dead?" Grant said.

My heart sank in my chest at the thought of poor Mrs. Ratchet waiting for Donald to wake up, only to end up with a stiff rotting corpse of a cat. It would be like a horror movie–old woman lives with cat corpse for days without realizing it! It would be awful.

"It's highly unlikely the flea control had any effect," Brian said. "It's likely Donald will be up and about very soon."

"But we have to make sure," Grant said.

"Agreed," Brian said. "After I dominate the world

we'll begin surveillance."

So we waited. Rudy and I went back to my house and sat on lawn chairs on the front porch, certain that as soon as Donald woke up, Mrs. Ratchet would put him out. Eventually all the kids ended up at my house for the afternoon—they weren't allowed inside; that was a big rule. The zombie cat virus was really bringing the neighborhood together. It was too bad the authorities would soon come and rope us off and we'd be stuck with one another all summer. I mean, voluntarily hanging out is one thing, but neighborhood prison? I wasn't looking forward to it.

We played kick ball in the street until my mom drove her car up the driveway.

We all stopped and looked over at Mrs. Ratchet's house. No Donald.

"What about the cats that never go out?" I said.

"What about them?" Brian said, his big alien eyes zooming in on my face.

"We...we," I stuttered under his gaze. "We couldn't treat them with the flea control."

Brian shook his head. "I really don't think it did any good, anyway."

I nodded and felt my cheeks flush. Maybe he was right. The little door far back in Mrs. Ratchet's gaping, empty garage opened and I saw her tired old body bent over, pushing Donald, tired, old, and bent just like her, out of the house. She stood up, somewhat, caught sight of us standing on my lawn watching her, and waved.

"Well, graduates," my mom said getting out of her car. "How does it feel?"

"Mom," I said with a roll of my eyes. "None of us graduated. We all have school next year."

"Even high school graduates go on to college," she said.

"By choice," Brian said.

Mom shook her head and walked into the garage to go into the house. I smiled at Brian and didn't even feel weird about it. Sometimes, lately, he didn't seem so scary.

"All right, guys," Rudy said.

"Excuse me?" Sarah said.

"Guys and...you people," he said. "Check on your cats and meet up in the oak lot after dinner."

"But," Natalie said, shoving a Ritz cracker into her mouth. She didn't finish, but I knew what she wanted to say.

"We agreed not to meet in the woods at night," I said. Right away I winced.

Sarah rolled her eyes at me. "Oh, grow up," she said. "It's the same woods whether it's dark or light."

I had the sinking feeling my summer was lost.

Chapter Fourteen

We all showed up that night after dinner, except Rudy. Natalie was eating a sandwich for dessert. Grant was jumping up and grabbing the lowest branch in the tree, hanging on, swinging a bit, and then falling back to the ground. He kept his eyes on me, smirking, because he knew I was too short to reach the branch. I thought maybe in two more years, I'd be able to do it. But the truth was I would never be as tall as Grant. I could tell.

"We'll wait for Rudy," I said.

Brian the Alien was walking a big circle at the outer edge of the oak, kicking at roots that poked up out of the dirt and thrashing the wild petunia and pennyroyal bushes with a stick he'd found.

"What for?" Grant said. "Let's do this thing."

"Do what?"

"Whatever is next. Antibiotics. Induced vomiting. Chopping off heads."

Brian and the girls laughed.

"We're not chopping off any heads," I said.

"Well, what else have you got in mind?" Natalie said.

"I don't know." I shrugged, feeling a bit stupid. "I think we should brainstorm some more."

Grant laughed and snorted. "You said *brain*storm."

I rolled my eyes. "What caused this virus and what might cure it? Clearly flea control has no effect."

"You want us to cure the virus?" Brian said.

"Come on, we only dosed them one time," Grant said. "We don't know if it might have some effect with more applications."

"You know," Natalie said, her curls bouncing with every snotty shake of her head. "You're not supposed to give cats that stuff more than once a month. You could make them very sick."

"Or kill them?" Grant said. "They're zombies!"

"That's no excuse for poisoning them with flea control," she said.

Grant shook his head. "I say we take the cats to the vet and explain what's been going on."

"Like they'd believe us," Brian said. "No, I'm with the kid. Let's see what we can figure out. Let's at least try. And if it doesn't work..."

"Quarantine," I said.

"You don't know they'll quarantine us," Sarah said.

"But it's contagious. It spread all through the neighborhood. The only reason no other cats have it is because our cats can't leave here. They're blocked in by the big roads, and the canal, and the fence. Don't you see?" I was getting dramatic now. "We're living in like, like a petri dish. And the virus is festering and spreading among us. And look at my arms!" I held out my forearms where the scratches were healing nicely. But I still winced at the thought. "How many of us were scratched? It's only a matter of time before we're all sick and the men in HazMat suits show up."

I could see fear finally light up in Sarah's eyes, but Brian and Grant just smirked.

Rudy walked into the clearing from the path carrying Busby, limp in his arms. "Well, he finally did it," Rudy said. He laid Busby down at the base of the oak trunk and wiped a tear from his eye. "I think it's for good this time."

"How'd he die?" Natalie said, stuffing the last of her sandwich in her mouth and wiping her sleeve across her face.

Rudy shook his head. "I don't know. I found him lying in the front yard."

"All right," Sarah said. "Now we keep watch."

"Huh?" Natalie said.

"We keep watch," she said. "That was Busby's ninth life. His last one. We want to see what happens. If he stays dead, we have nothing to worry about, right?"

"Nothing to worry about?" Rudy said.

"Yeah. If he's dead, then the cats will die after their ninth lives. It will all be over."

"But our cats will be dead," Natalie whimpered.

Sarah put her hands on her hips and glared at her. "I don't like it any more than you do. But at least we'll know they're not zombies."

"But what about us?" I said. "Look at my arms!"

"Oh, cut it out," Sarah said. "There's no need to panic...yet."

"All right, all right," I said. "And if he doesn't stay dead?"

"If he doesn't, we have to figure something else out," Grant said.

"We should keep an eye on him out here in the

woods," Brian said. "In case he wakes up violent, as I predict."

"Great," Grant said, strangely cheerful. "We'll take the night shifts."

"No fair," Rudy balked.

"Like Dad's going to let you spend the night out here in the woods," Grant said.

"I bet he would. We can camp out."

"Well, how many nights are we going to wait?" Natalie said. "He's going to start getting stinky and, you know, rotty."

"One or two nights ought to do it," Brian said.

"I'm asking Dad," Rudy said.

"Fine," Grant said. "For tomorrow night. Tonight, we're staying out here without you little twits." He grinned at Brian and they both took the path, eager to pack their camping gear.

"Okay, I'm thinking that's a little weird," Sarah said. "They shouldn't be so excited to spend the night with a dead cat."

Chapter Fifteen

It wasn't technically summer yet. It was still the last day of school. The next day would be my first full day of living alone. Well, if you could call it that. And I was calling it that. Every morning, after mom left, I had to walk Pearl over to Katy's house where she'd spend the day. Then I had to check in at Mrs. Ratchet's. Then I was on my own until lunch, when my mom or dad would come home to check in on me. The rule was, I had to be there. If I wasn't, they were calling out the National Guard and boy would I be in big trouble. And then I had to check in again with Mrs. Ratchet every afternoon at three o'clock. Piece of cake! I was a man! Practically a bachelor. Except for my Aunt Candy. I forgot about my Aunt Candy. She was the morning drop in. She had a key so I had to leave a note if I wasn't going to be there. And my Uncle Roy was supposed to stop by unexpectedly two or three times a week. You know, sometimes I got the feeling my parents didn't trust me, on my own, in their house.

Even so, I was still rather free for the summer, at least until we headed out to Gram's condo in Melbourne Beach. And I was determined to figure out this cat crisis so I wouldn't miss out on two weeks of ocean, sun, seaweed, and sea gulls. I could hardly sleep that night thinking about it—that and Busby. And maybe the scratches on my arms that could possibly turn me into a zombie.

In a way—and don't tell Rudy I said this—I really hoped Busby wouldn't wake up. I wish I could say it was because it would mean this would all be over and even though it was likely all of our cats would die and we'd be really sad all summer, it would also mean I might not become a zombie. Then again, there were no assurances.

But the real reason I hoped Busby didn't wake up was because if he didn't, I would get to ask permission to sleep out in the woods the next night. Somehow I knew my parents wouldn't give in to that. It was enough that I was allowed to stay home sort of alone this summer. Sleeping out in the woods behind Rudy's was probably too much to hope for.

The phone started ringing as soon as my mom's car was backing out of the driveway the next morning.

"Come on, come on," Rudy was yelling when I answered. "Where are you?"

Sheesh, didn't he sleep at all? He was not happy to find out he'd have to wait for me to drop Pearl off and check in at Mrs. Ratchet's. I left a note for Aunt Candy on the kitchen table and ran as fast as I could, dragging Pearl along on the first leg of my journey, speeding back down Sea Gull to Ratchet's and breathlessly checking in: Did we clean up after breakfast? Yes, Mrs. Ratchet. Did we make sure the cats were let out? Yes, ma'am. And Pearl was dropped off to Mrs. Stoddard and no one else? Yes. She held out an old wrinkled hand and said, "Pinky swear." I had to smile. Mrs. Ratchet was okay. And finally, to Rudy's house. Natalie was already there. I wanted to sit down and rest, but Rudy wouldn't let me. He dragged us into the woods right away.

"He must still be dead, Rudy," I said, trying to ease the blow. "He'd have come home last night if he woke up."

"Maybe," he said.

We trudged along the path through the empty lot and entered the clearing where the big oak stood, pushing all the other trees and shrubs out of its way with its long bushy arms. Grant and Brian were in sleeping bags on the ground under the old tree. Grant's mouth was open and he was snoring. Brian's glasses weren't on his face, which struck me as odd, even though, when I thought about it, I mean, who wears their glasses when they sleep?

"There he is," Rudy called excitedly and I heard a muted, hoarse meow.

Busby was sitting on a low branch, deep red eyes taking us in hungrily. He meowed again. It was awful, much worse than before. He sounded aged, creaky, raspy. His fur looked as if it had been dragged through a muddy ditch and one ear was pulled back as if he were half-angry. His tail didn't twitch so much as it shuddered. Then he started hacking. *Brawk. Brawk.*

"Watch it," Rudy said. "He's going to spew."

Chapter Sixteen

We stepped back and sure enough, Busby leaned his head over the edge of the branch and puked out a big, soggy, hair ball. It landed, *thwap*, on the dirt next to Grant.

"Why didn't he go home?" Natalie said. "If I was sick, I'd want to be at home."

"Beats me," Rudy said.

"Are you serious?" I said. "Look at him. He's a zombie. Zombies don't go home."

"But he looks really hungry," Rudy said. "And home's where the food bowl is." He looked at me hopefully.

"He just puked up a hair ball the size of Pluto. And even if he was hungry, he wouldn't want kibble," I was nearly in a panic. "He wants brains."

Natalie pulled a baggie stuffed with several Pop Tart pieces from her pants pocket and opened it up.

"I don't think cats eat those," Rudy said.

"They're not for him." She shoved half a Pop Tart

into her mouth.

"He'll want brains, not sugar," I said.

Rudy nodded but I knew he wasn't listening.

"Let's try to feed him, then," he said. "Let's go get some food from my house."

"We can't leave him here with them," I said, pointing to the snoozing teens. "He might try to eat their brains."

Rudy and Natalie just looked at me. Grant let out a long, deep throated snore.

"Alfie," Natalie said and swallowed, "you really think a cat can get into a human skull?"

I stared at her with my mouth open. Then I gave up and we trudged slowly to Rudy's where he went inside to get a bowl full of food. By the time we got back to the clearing, Natalie was almost finished with her Pop Tarts and Grant had woken up. He kicked Brian, who sat upright suddenly and yelped.

"He's alive again," Rudy said.

"We know." Grant yawned. "He woke up early last night."

"Why didn't you come home and tell me?" Rudy said.

"What for?"

"Well, I brought him some food. Maybe he'll come down now."

Rudy tried to tempt Busby down with the food, but Busby just sat and stared at him.

"*Meeeowaaaallll*," he said. It was horrible.

"Maybe he's scared to come down with all of us here," Brian said, sliding his thick glasses onto his nose.

"He's never been scared of us before," Rudy said.

The Alien shrugged. "Well, at least we know we still have a problem."

"What are we going to do?" I said.

We all stared, our gazes darting back and forth from one face to another searching for some sense of the situation. But there was none.

"He looks really dirty," Natalie said. "Isn't he cleaning himself?"

"Maybe they have some kind of skin condition," I said. "My grandma had a dog once with a skin condition. He had patches of red, bald spots all over him. And he smelled."

"Our cats definitely smell," Natalie said.

Sarah came along the path singing about shoes or something and smiled really big when we all turned to look at her. She finished the song and bowed. Girls. Here we had a deadly zombie cat infestation and she's showing off. Still, she froze, her mouth open, when she saw Busby in the tree. "What is that?"

"It's Busby," I said.

Sarah shook her head in disbelief. "That is not a cat." Then she smiled and laughed and nudged Natalie.

"Don't tease him," Natalie said eyeing Busby. "Poor thing."

"Your cats are going to look just like him if we can't figure this thing out," I said.

"Are you sure that was his last life, Rudy?" Sarah said.

Rudy nodded. "Pretty sure."

"Then what are we going to do now?"

"We thought it might be a skin problem. They need ointment or something."

"But if Busby has gone full zombie," Brian said, "we shouldn't get anywhere near him."

"Well, what if we spray them with cortisone spray?" Grant said.

We all looked at him dumbly.

"Maybe they have a rash." He smiled. "We have

spray in the garage," he said, apologetically.

"Is there anything you don't have in your garage?" I said.

Armed with twelve cans of cortisone spray—a full case, fifty percent off with a dollar off coupon—we traipsed around the neighborhood calling cats and spraying them down. Surprisingly enough, cats don't like to get sprayed with stuff. They don't even like the cans.

I stood out on the back porch and shook my can up and Fletch and Gnarly jumped out of the chairs they were sleeping in and darted under the table. It was as if they'd had a bad experience with a spray can before. I wasn't deterred. I crawled under the table and started spraying. And I closed my eyes and screamed because a nice breeze was wafting through the screens turning the spray back onto my face. I couldn't say for sure if the cats got any or not, but they didn't look wet with cortisone, so I followed them across the porch to the fake potted plants.

You can't have real potted plants on the porch because the cats will eat them. Even if they're not poisonous, you don't want your cats eating plants. Take my word for it; my mom tried it. She researched it on the computer and everything, and went shopping with a big list of plants that wouldn't kill a cat if he ate them. And she made my dad lift seven or so heavy—what she called decorative—pots into shopping carts, along with a few huge bags of potting soil, and somehow I knew I wasn't going to get off without getting dirty.

I worked all day potting those stupid plants. And what happened? Fletch chewed on them and then spit up bits of twig and leaf and green foam all over the porch and house—and the yard, too, once my mom caught him and threw him out.

"That's it," she yelled and made my dad haul the heavy potted plants outside the screened porch and out by the back fence. And you know what? That dumb cat never ate those plants again. What was that all about? Do you suppose he figured that because they were in the house, assuming a cat would think the back porch was part of the house anyway, they were food? And when they were outside, they were just plants? Maybe. Fletch and Gnarly both eat grass and puke. But they don't touch those plants.

So, my mom put some fake plants in their place, for what she calls ambiance. And whenever one side gets all chewed up–because, yes, Fletch chews on them, too; but he doesn't barf up the pieces–she turns the chewed part to the screen so she can't see it. She's only got one or two turns left, I'd say.

And that's where I caught them–between two large pots, filled with plastic Ficus and hydrangea, and the screen. I sprayed and sprayed until they were definitely medicated. If nothing else, they wouldn't itch for the rest of the week.

"Hah!" I said to them. That was much easier than the flea control. And I still had some of the cortisone left.

Chapter Seventeen

We were supposed to meet out by the oak again after we sprayed the cats on our lists but when I came to the end of the path, I saw Alien Watley, alone, walking around under the tree, his hands shoved into his jeans pocket, kicking at roots. My heart pounded heavy in my chest and I was screaming at myself in my head. Turn around, I was saying. Run! And before he saw me, I managed to back slowly away and behind the knot of pines. Then I turned and ran smack into Natalie, knocking her napkin full of tiny pretzels out of her hand. She screamed as the pretzels flew into the air and scattered into the bushes.

"That was my snack," she said. "What's the matter with you?"

"*Shh*," I said. "He'll hear you."

Rudy came along, laughing and trying to tell us something about the cortisone spray and his neighbor's cats. Then Grant was on the trail with us and I felt like

I was being dragged along before I could catch my breath.

"Little twit," Grant said, putting me into a light choke hold. "You look sick. You didn't swallow any of the spray did you? I don't think you're supposed to do that."

"No, it's nothing. I'm cool."

But I held back on the trail and Rudy walked with me.

"You look like you saw a demon or something. Are your cats okay?"

"I almost got murdered," I said. "That's all."

Rudy stopped walking. "What?"

"I showed up by the oak and nobody was there but the Alien. He could have murdered me and dragged my body over to the ditch behind the Ricker's before you guys showed up."

"Is that all?"

"Isn't that enough?"

Rudy shook his head. "I'm sure he isn't really a murderer."

"Oh, he's a murderer all right," I said.

Rudy grabbed my shoulders and gave me a violent shake. "Snap out of it."

And I did. "Sorry," I mumbled. "I don't know what got into me."

"You found yourself alone with The Alien. It could happen to anybody. But you're safe now. So be cool."

"I feel like I escaped death."

"*Nah*. At worst, a pounding."

"Well, I wouldn't want to experience that either."

"Course not. Who would?"

We walked the rest of the path and came out under the oak to find everyone sitting under it, except Sarah.

"Anybody seen her?" Grant said. We all shook our

heads.

"She has a lot of cats to spray," Rudy said. "I should have helped her."

"Well, I don't think it worked, anyway," Natalie said. "There's too much fur."

Suddenly, Sarah came off the path, panting; she bent over and put her hands on her knees. I'd never seen her so disheveled. Well, there was that time we all got to ride in Mrs. Hurley's convertible.

"Natalie's right," she said. "I tried rubbing it all in, but Poochie died anyway."

"What?" We all seemed to say it at once.

"I lathered him up and he walked across the street and lay down in the grass in Mr. Philips' yard. He died. Just up and died. I picked him up and carried him home and put him on the front porch. And when I got finished with the other cats, I went back and he was alive again. He looks awful. Not as bad as Busby. But still. He's a zombie. I'm telling you; one of my cats is a zombie."

"What if you killed him?" Natalie said. Sarah glared at her. "No offense. But...with the cortisone?"

"I didn't kill any of the other cats."

"Mine didn't die either," I said.

"It didn't do anything," Grant said. "It didn't kill them and it didn't cure them."

"What do we do now?" There was a definite whine in Natalie's voice.

"We have to chop off their heads," Grant said. "There's no other way."

"I am not chopping off my cats' heads," Sarah said. "I don't think I could do it."

"Brian will do it," Grant said, looking at the Alien. "You can do it, right?"

We were all staring at him and I don't know about

the others, but I thought I was going to jump out of my own skin the way he looked back at us. One of his eyebrows was lifted and his mouth was twisted up in an evil kind of smirk. It was as if he was thinking how much he would love to murder our cats and chop off their heads. But hey, someone was going to have to do it and who better than a person who likes that sort of thing?

"Fine," Brian said. "But we haven't exhausted all of our options."

"Oh, yeah?" I said, my voice quavering like a terrified child's. "What else can we do?"

"Catnip."

"Catnip?" Sarah said.

"Yes. Catnip. It's a drug, you know? For cats, anyway. And it's not harmful to them, since they're all adults. We should give it a try."

"What do you expect it to do?" Grant said.

"It's worth a shot," Brian said.

"I agree," Natalie said. "We have to try everything. I mean..."

"I say we go for it," Sarah said. She pushed her glasses up her nose. "I don't want my cats to lose their heads before we've done everything we can think of."

"Does your mom buy catnip in bulk?" I asked Rudy.

"As a matter of fact..."

Chapter Eighteen

As it turned out, some months before, the local dollar store moved from a smaller space to a larger one. And they had an incredible blow-out sale before they moved. Their biggest customer was, of course, Mrs. Albee. There was a box full of fabric mice filled with catnip somewhere in the Albee's garage and Rudy and I were sent to find it.

Because all of the cats in the neighborhood kept climbing stacks in Rudy's garage to get at it, the box full of toy mice was triple taped, and on top of a shelf of canned goods standing against one wall. Rudy and I stood in the aisle with the step stool, the heavy metal shelf on one side and stacks of charcoal bags, stinky fertilizer, and bedspreads in funny square plastic zipper bags on the other. That's right. Rudy's mom bought six big bedspreads at a flea market two years ago because... well, because; and they've been stacked in two columns next to the fertilizer ever since.

"I'm not tall enough," Rudy said, staring up at the

box on the top shelf. Even with the step stool, he'd never reach it.

"Me either," I said. "Let's get your brother."

"*Nah*," he said. "I don't want to go all the way out back again. Climb on my shoulders."

"Are you out of your mind?"

"No, just do it." He knelt in front of the stool.

"You can't carry my weight."

"Sure I can," he said. "And you can hold onto the shelf to keep steady. I won't drop you. I promise."

I can't say for sure how it is that Rudy gets me into these things. My mother often says I don't have a lick of sense and while I'm not exactly sure what that means, I'm going to have to admit it's true. I climbed onto Rudy's shoulders and held on to the shelf for dear life while he fell into it trying to stand with me on his back.

"See," he wheezed. "Easy peasy."

"Now you have to climb onto the step stool," I reminded him.

"No problem."

When he put his right foot on the first step, we both grabbed onto the shelf and he pulled himself up. The shelf tilted toward us.

"*Ayah!*" Rudy let go and stepped off the stool, falling backward into the stacks of bedspreads. Naturally I fell into the fertilizer.

"Okay, okay," he said. "I think I got it."

So we tried again and this time Rudy used the shelf only to steady himself, not pull. It's a shame these things can't be worked out ahead of time. It wasn't so bad. There was only a little bit of poopy smelling fertilizer on the bags when I landed on them and the odor mostly wore off by the time we got back out to the old oak tree.

Once we'd opened the little packages of catnip mice, Natalie had a great idea.

"We need to focus on a few cats this time," she said. "If I try to do something with Mrs. Swanson's cat again, she might call the cops."

"Good idea," the Alien said. "Let's stick with Sarah's, Alf's, and Busby. That's enough of a sample."

Sarah and Natalie went to Sarah's house to make sure all of her cats got at least one fabric mouse and Rudy and I went to his house first. We found Busby out back sitting under a tree looking dead. His fur was mussed and sticking out all over in odd directions, like he'd given up on grooming completely. One eye was closed up a bit and the tip of his tongue was hanging out the front of his mouth. We approached easily. Rudy got ahead of me and I reached out and pulled him back by the arm. You never knew when one of them was going to leap onto your head and start gnashing at your skull.

"Busby," Rudy said. "Put your tongue back in."

Busby didn't do it. He just sat there watching us.

"Well, go on," I said. "Toss him a mouse."

Rudy threw a few fabric mice onto the grass in front of Busby and we watched as he sniffed the air around them. Then he let out a low, scratchy meow, sniffed some more and finally walked over and fell on top of them. He rolled this way and that, pulled one into his mouth and gnawed on it, drooling.

"All right," Rudy said. "Your house."

My cats were on the back porch and while they didn't look as bad as Busby, I thought they were looking worse than they should. At least they kept their tongues inside their mouths. They did the same with their mice, rolling all over them, chewing them, and slobbering.

"It's kind of gross, isn't it?" Rudy said.

And so we all waited. Grant and the Alien played Risk over at Rudy's with their friends Tim and Drake Goodall. Grant swore they would only tell them about our zombie cat problem if they would swear an oath to secrecy. Turns out they didn't believe him. But Tim and Drake Goodall were older–off at college. I always got the feeling they thought even Grant and Brian were just kids. And I have to be honest...zombie cats? It's not an easy thing to accept when you hear it from Grant Albee.

Rudy and I and the girls played kick ball in the street. Then we walked over behind the Ricker's to see if there were any frogs in the ditch and Sarah got dried mud on her shoes and blamed Rudy. Then we shot hoops over at Natalie's and she won HORSE. Finally we decided to walk to the convenience store because Nat wanted Twinkies.

We walked through the empty lot and crawled through the hole in the fence only to come upon Mr. Tanturo on his hands and knees at the trunk of his largest oak tree. When he saw us, he staggered to his feet.

"What are you kids doing here? Were you spying on me?"

"No, sir," Natalie said. "Not at all."

We apologized and ran along the back of the fence to Linda Percy's yard. Her family didn't mind us cutting through their side yard to get to the street. At the store, Natalie got two packs of Twinkies and I got a candy bar. On the way back, we all argued about whether or not our four streets were part of a larger neighborhood that included the curvy roads on the other side of the canal and the fancy streets named after golfers. I voted no–they're three separate neighborhoods. But Sarah said it was all the same. It almost came to blows. It was nearly as bad as the time we argued about whether the toilet paper was supposed to come off the roll from the top or the bottom.

When we got to the hole in the fence leading into our own neighborhood, Mr. Tanturo was still in his back yard. This time, he was on a step stool, hanging what looked like a pine cone from one of the oak branches. I'd have got a better look if he hadn't started yelling again. He was so upset with us, he fell off the stool. But he landed on his feet.

"I told you before to stop coming over here. You're bringing those filthy gray squirrels with you."

It was always best not to listen to Mr. Tanturo. Rudy and I learned a long time ago to just apologize, or yell, and get back through the hole. But I guess Natalie didn't have the same teacher we did.

"We didn't bring any squirrels with us," she told him.

"I know you're doing it. You're sending them over. They've chased off all my squirrels. I don't want your squirrels. Wrong sorts of squirrels."

"Maybe they're coming through the hole in the fence," she said.

"They are not," he said. "I watch that hole day and night. No. You bring 'em through. Under your shirts or in your socks. I know it."

Rudy pulled at Natalie. "Let's go. We're sorry, Mr. Tanturo. We won't bring squirrels with us."

"Didn't anybody ever tell you not to talk to crazy people?" I asked Natalie.

She smiled. "But they're the most fun kind."

"*Shh*," Rudy said. "Somebody's in trouble."

Turns out it was Sarah. Her mother's screams echoed through the neighborhood. Sarah's eyes grew as wide as pepperoni pizzas and we ran to her house as fast as we could. I just knew we were going to find all of her cats dead and her mother traumatized. Instead, when we walked in the front room, we found her mother picking up cats. She had two, one under each arm.

"Close that door!" she screamed. "Don't let any of them back in. Who gave the cats catnip? Were you out of your mind? Look at my house. Just look at it. Slobber everywhere." She went to the front door, managed to pry it open while carrying the cats, and tossed them out. "Everywhere!"

"That's sort of gross," Natalie said.

And the catnip didn't even work. Gnarly turned up dead that night. One of Sarah's cats and one of Natalie's, too. I couldn't believe I was going to have to choose between going to the beach and letting the Alien chop off my cats' heads or staying home and being quarantined, waiting to turn into a zombie. You might think that's an easy choice. But it's not.

Chapter Nineteen

Grant was ready for the head chopping ceremony, but the rest of us still resisted. There had to be something that would fix this thing. And anyway, I reminded him, if we found a cure for cat zombie syndrome, we could be rich selling our information and research to the United Nations; they could use it to come up with a cure for human zombie syndrome.

"Why would you assume there is a link between the two?" Brian said.

"Well, there could be," I said.

"The little twit is right," Grant said. "We should keep doing our research."

So we sat under the oak tree in the woods for an hour or so trying to decide what to do next. Natalie handed a bag of cookies around and we all munched and thought and thought and munched.

"You know," she said, smacking her hands together to rid them of cookie crumbs, "my mom used to feed our cats tuna fish a lot until the vet said to stop. He said she was giving them too much."

"Tuna has a lot of mercury in it," Brian the Alien said. "It can cause mercury poisoning if they get too much."

"But," Rudy said, "is there something in tuna cats need? Maybe our cats aren't getting enough of it?"

Brian pinched his face up, thinking. "Well, cats need taurine. It's an amino acid. And it's in tuna fish. But they ought to be getting that in their food."

"But lately, we've all been getting discount cat food from a sale Mrs. Albee scored," I said. "Maybe it doesn't have this taurine stuff in it."

"It's possible."

"But we don't want to poison the cats with tuna," Sarah said.

"A little won't hurt," Brian said. "And if it works, it means we have to convince your parents to choose a better cat food. Or get a supplement."

And so it was decided. Rudy and I were sent to the garage again, this time for four cans of tuna fish—a half can for each of the cats in our research sample. This time, Sarah, Rudy, and I worked together because Sarah said she'd have to separate her cats to make sure Piggles didn't eat all of Clementine's or Poochie's food. Piggles came by his name honestly.

The cats weren't nearly as appreciative of the tuna as I expected. I mean, it was supposed to be a special treat. Seafood. Real seafood. Even I didn't get to go out to eat at Red Lobster more than once a year. Here they were getting half a can, and Busby turned up his nose, stuck his tongue out, and sniffed. But after some prodding, and Rudy slathering a piece of tuna on his whiskers, he finally ate it.

Gnarly and Fletch weren't much nicer about it. At

least they ate it. But they kept looking up at me, as if waiting for me to go away so they could barf the tuna into one of the potted plants. Sarah's six cats were more interested, but Piggles didn't try to eat any of the other cats' tuna.

"Piggles has only died twice," Sarah said. "I thought he'd be the healthiest and try to eat all of it." She sighed.

"Don't worry," I said. "We'll figure this out."

But instead of figuring anything out, the mystery only got deeper. That night after dinner, we all gathered in the woods under the old oak with our flashlights, stinking of mosquito repellent and tuna juice. It was only supposed to be a quick meeting to check in and see if any of the cats died. But when Rudy showed up with Grant, he called us all to follow them and be very quiet.

"What is it?" I whispered.

"The cats," Grant said. "There's something wrong with them."

"Uh...*duh*," Natalie said. "Zombies."

"Something else."

Grant and Rudy led us to the edge of their back yard and across to Mr. Haggerty's where we all stopped, stunned. There were our cats. All of them. Plus some. Gnarly, Fletch, Busby, Piggles, Poochie, and the rest of Sarah's cats. Donald. Fluffy. The Goodall's cat, Silk. And more. They were walking into the empty lot behind Mr. Haggerty's. But not orderly. Not straight. They were wandering in different directions. Slowly. They turned back, and then back again. But their general, albeit roundabout, forward movement was taking them into the empty lot.

"Where are they going?"

"Maybe they're just out and about," Grant said.

"Are you crazy?" Sarah said. "Cats don't go out and about."

"Don't they?" Grant said. "Like you and Nat go to the mall, or ride your bikes around the neighborhood? Nothing like that?"

"No," Natalie said. "Cats prowl and hunt and find places to sleep. They don't go out and about. Especially with other cats."

I didn't want to say anything, because, well, by then we were all sure we were in the middle of a terrifying zombie cat outbreak, but truthfully, this was not the first time our cats had gotten together. It was weird that they were in the woods staggering about; I'll give you that. But when I had a chance to think about it, why wouldn't they? There were times when some of our cats would run together through the neighborhood chasing squirrels and climbing trees. They fought sometimes and chased one another away other times, but they all knew one another.

"Okay, that's it," Brian the Alien said. He shined his flashlight at the cats and they turned toward us, their eyes glowing red. One of them let out an angry, howling meow. Brian clicked off his flashlight leaving us standing in the dark, the sound of padding cat feet in our ears. "There is definitely something wrong with the cats in our neighborhood."

"You think?" Natalie said.

We watched as the shadowy cats disappeared into the woods.

"We should follow them," Brian said.

"Are you out of your mind?" Rudy said. "They're probably off to a zombie cat meeting where they'll be sharing tips on cracking into human skulls."

"Oh, come on," Sarah said.

"He has a point," I said. Somewhere in the woods

we heard a guttural meow. "I swear Gnarly tried to get into mine."

"Let's go," Grant said. "Everybody stay quiet. Brian can use his flashlight, but only him. We don't want to freak them out.'

So, against my better judgement, I followed the others tiptoeing into the woods after the neighborhood cats. They didn't seem to mind. In fact, they didn't seem to know we were there. But then, they are cats and frankly, cats are pretty independent. I have a feeling if my mom didn't feed Gnarly and Fletch, they wouldn't pay us any attention at all.

Another deep, raspy meow echoed through the muggy night air. When we got to the back of the empty lot, the cats disappeared, one by one, through the hole in the wooden fence, into Mr. Tanturo's yard. We stood in a row facing the fence, a pale yellow circle of light from the Alien's flashlight glowing on the wood slats.

"I'm not going in there," I said. "If Mr. Tanturo catches us in his backyard at night, he'll think we really are changing out his squirrels."

A hissing screech pierced the night and then a melodic growl. More growls joined in and suddenly a chorus of screaming–awful, terrible, painful howling– echoed from behind the fence.

"Cat fight," Grant said. He looked at all of us down the row. He was scared; we all were.

"They're killing each other," Natalie said, barely heard over the din.

"It's just like Mrs. Wilkinson's favorite word," I shouted.

They all turned to me then and I knew I'd said something stupid. But that was all I could think of. Mrs. Wilkinson's favorite word. She taught sixth grade

English. We all had her class. And she made everyone find a favorite word. The cats were shrieking and howling and suddenly Mr. Tanturo yelped and swore and a screened door slammed. It was a cacophony. That's what it was. Cacophony. Mrs. Wilkinson said it over and over again. Such a lovely word, she said. And I had to wonder if Mrs. Wilkinson had ever actually heard one because all that screaming and howling was not lovely at all.

When something thumped against the other side of the fence, I turned and ran. I'd like to say someone else did it first and it's possible, because we were all running, but I probably started it. We ran through the empty lot, into Mr. Haggerty's back yard straight through to the front. And then we dispersed. That was my favorite word last year. I didn't hear any good-byes and I didn't care. I ran all the way home and into the living room past the den, into my room, and behind the bed. I sat huddled on the floor, catching my breath.

"What on earth?" my mother said coming around the side of my bed. She looked at my face, the terror on my face, crossed her arms over her middle and sighed. "Ghost stories in the woods again? Honestly, when will you boys learn?"

"Mom," I said, breathless and spooky. "Our cats. The cats. All of them. Zombies."

She smirked. "Good one."

"No, no. Mom. Really. They keep dying and coming back to life. They're ratty looking. Tongues! Sticking out."

"That would explain all the drool on the sofa."

"Now they're out in the woods, screaming. The screaming!" I slapped my hands over my ears. "Our cats are zombies. I'm telling you. Zombies!"

Her mouth turned up into one of those really

proud mom smiles. And she shook her head in that my-boy-is-so-adorable nod. "You really need to write fiction, Alfie. What an imagination."

"You'll see," I mumbled as she left the room. "You'll all see."

Chapter Twenty

But they didn't see. I slept on the floor by my bed. With my bedroom door closed. If Gnarly clawed at my head that night, I'd have screamed and ran through the house, and probably been grounded. Best not take any chances, right?

The next morning I was bleary eyed. Exhausted. But I had to get up to see my parents off to work and handle my responsibilities as a bachelor. More important, I was waiting for my parents and Pearl to see that Gnarly and Fletch were missing. And when I saw the two cats on the back porch waiting to be fed, I hoped they'd see their rattiness, their tongues hanging out, or...something. Something that says, "We're zombies."

But there they sat–perfectly normal, well-behaved, hungry cats.

"There are your zombies," my dad said. He gave me a fatherly punch on the arm.

"Mom told you, huh?"

"What do you think?" he said. "Dare you go out

onto the porch and pour the kibble?"

I sighed. And then I went to the laundry room to get out the plastic canister. Darn zombie cats. Out on the porch, I could feel my family's eyes on me as I poured kibble into Gnarly and Fletch's bowls. Fletch purred and walked up against my leg.

"Sure, sure," I told them. "You act normal now. But you're not fooling me. Not one bit. I know what you are."

They put their faces into their bowls as soon as the kibbles tinkled in.

"Zombies," I whispered.

I think I jumped three feet straight up when the thunder crashed. It rattled the sliding glass door and brought out a yelp from Pearl. It was only then I noticed the gray sky; I guess I thought it was just my lack of sleep that had made the day so dim. My mom drove Pearl down to Katy's in case the rain started and I ran over to Mrs. Ratchet's to check in.

"Got an umbrella?" she said.

I held it up with a smile.

"Cats fed? Pearl dropped off?"

"Yes, Ma'am."

And I was off to Rudy's. We were all shocked when Sarah showed up in the empty lot by the oak. She doesn't do rain. Something about her hair. And you might think I'm being dramatic, but when she walked off the path toward us wearing that silly purple plastic hat, and even Natalie gasped at seeing her, I started trembling. There's something really wrong in the world when Sarah Johnston comes outside on a day like that. Thunder shook the sky above us.

"Well, clearly, eating tuna had no effect on the cats," Brian the Alien said.

"Did any die?" Natalie said. She had a baggie of dry

cereal, but instead of eating it, was clutching it to her chest with both hands.

We all shook our heads.

"Doesn't matter," Rudy said. "Last night...what they were doing."

Brian nodded. "They're not right. Not right at all."

"So, it's head chopping time?" Grant said, too cheerful. He slapped Brian on the back. "Got an ax? I bet you do."

"No," I said. "I mean, it's not like they've killed anybody." I couldn't believe I was saying that. My vacation at Gram's condo on the beach started soon. But I could feel it, then, in my gut–I had to admit it–I was willing to sacrifice my trip to the beach to keep Gnarly and Fletch from getting their heads chopped. "We have to keep trying."

Brian nodded and I felt my whole body relax. Maybe the Alien wasn't a bloodthirsty killer after all.

A wind picked up in the branches of the pines and oaks above us.

"It's going to rain all day, today," Sarah said and winced. "It'll start soon."

"That's it," Grant said.

"What's it?" Rudy said.

"The rain."

We all stared at him.

"I've been thinking about it, almost from the start. I might have the answer."

"Well, go on then," Natalie said.

Rudy and I turned to her, surprised, and I wondered if he was thinking the same thing I was...how we were all getting more used to being around Grant and Brian. I mean, really. We were standing in the woods, not two feet from Brian 'The Alien' Watley, talking to him like his equal–like he wasn't going to body slam us against a tree at any second. It was all so weird. So unnerving. It made me wonder if there wasn't something wrong with *us*, more than the cats.

"I noticed Busby's fur right away," Grant was saying. "And I don't know if you guys noticed, but, well, he stinks."

"It's true," Sarah said. "The cats stink. And the tuna didn't help."

"Right," Grant said. "So I've been thinking Busby needed a bath."

"A bath?" I was stunned. And then I laughed. Loud.

My mom and dad tried to give Fletch a bath once. He was barely a year old, so not so big. He got into some fertilizer, probably in the Albee's yard, and smelled like poopy chemicals. My mom shrieked and said, "Bath!" My dad protested, but finally agreed. They ran nice warm water in the tub while Pearl and I, about three and six at the time, stood and watched from the hallway. Dad left the bathroom and came back with Fletch. Our mom was on her knees in front of the tub and Dad put Fletch in.

What followed plays out like a horror film in my mind. You ever watch those? The worst scenes—you know, where the bad guy starts doing his bad guy thing—are flashy. There's light and dark and screaming and suddenly the screen goes black. Right? It was just like that. Only instead of the screen going black, somehow the bathroom door got slammed shut and everything went silent as Fletch darted between Pearl and me. I could hear his claws scrambling on the kitchen tiles behind us as he made his sharp turn before pouncing out onto the back porch and he was gone. He didn't come home for days.

"People don't bathe cats," I said. "Cats clean themselves."

"Not these cats," the Alien said.

"He's right. They could all stand a scrubbing."

"But they're zombies," Rudy said. "We can't get near them."

"Long brushes," Grant said, beaming.

"Okay, let me see if I have this straight," I said. "You want us to put our cats in the bathtub? All by ourselves? And somehow make them stay in there while we scrub them with...toilet brushes?"

"No, little twit. No," Grant said. "The rain. We'll use the rain."

"Oh, that's much better," I said and snorted. "We put our cats out in the rain where they're just going to stand there while we soap them up and scrub them with toilet brushes."

"He's got a point," the Alien said.

I flushed all over. It was just plain weird to have the Alien agree with me. I thought I was saved at that point–thought I'd made it clear that bathing cats was something people in hazmat suits or armor did. But at that moment, Donald, Mrs. Ratchet's cat, stumbled through the clearing. We all stood there, thunder pounding the air around us, wind whooshing the trees, while the cat walked past us, real slow and determined, not noticing us at all.

When Donald finally disappeared into the woods again, on his way into Mr. Tanturo's neighborhood we assumed, Grant nodded and said, "See there. Easy as cake. They're little zombies. Totally out of it."

The Alien sighed and tilted his head. "It does seem possible."

"It's worth a try," Sarah said. "Right, Alfie? A try?"

And so I nodded. And I suppose they were right. Outside, at least, the cat could run away. There wouldn't be all that splashing and clawing up a person's arm trying to scramble out of a slippery bathtub, finally resorting to leaping onto another person's head and holding on for dear life only to be tossed away before the screen goes black.

Yes. It could work.

Chapter Twenty-one

The bathing of the cats would surely come to be legend, not only in our four-street neighborhood surrounded by ditches and woods. No...it would be legendary in the entire town of Palm Gardens. Maybe even the whole state of Florida. Teachers would tell students about the foolishness of running around in the rain in the summer, lowering your body's resistance to germs. Parents would scold their children against going out in thunderstorms by saying, remember Bird Place! But mayors and governors would pin Bird Place medals on other kids' chests for bravery against all odds, for doing what is right in the face of stormy weather. Generals would hand out commendations for going above and beyond the call of duty. We were going to be famous. We bathed undead cats in the rain!

We thought we'd have to scoot the cats out of our houses. We wanted to be prepared, so we decided to start in, you guessed it, the Albee's garage. But once we got to Rudy's front yard, we realized our job would be easier than expected. We saw cats. In the street. In the yards. Milling around, unsteady, confused...zombie cats.

"They're going out to the woods again," Grant said. "I bet that's it. They're going back to Mr. Tanturo's."

"Why?" Natalie said.

"Who knows? Who cares? Let's get the stuff."

Just inside the maze that is Rudy's garage, we found liquid dish soap and tiny paper drink cups and a box of discount toilet brushes. Thunder roared again and then all went quiet for two seconds before the downpour hit.

"Grant," Brian called over the clattering echo of rain. "Go out and see where the cats are."

I tried to stop him. It was pointless. Surely the cats had scattered as soon as the rain started. We could only hope they all went home and we'd find them cowering in garages and on back porches.

"So, what's the plan?" Natalie said.

"Some of us will dump cups of soap on them and others will follow with the brushes."

I shook my head, doubting once again.

"Come on, Alfie," Sarah said, yelling. "If you can chase a cat all over my roof, you can chase one in the rain." She handed me a toilet brush.

Brian turned toward the driveway and took off his glasses for a few seconds to clean them on his shirt. As he put them back on and squinted, the rest of us turned to see Grant, standing in the downpour, drenched, paralyzed with fear. We called to him, but he wouldn't come out of the rain.

"Somebody's going to have to go get him," I said, turning to Rudy.

"Why me?" Rudy's voice was suddenly high-pitched and squeaky.

"He's your brother," I said.

"Exactly. He won't listen to me."

"Brian, you're the strongest," Sarah said. "He'll have to be dragged."

"Hurry," I said. "Somebody go get him."

We watched as Brian darted out into the pouring rain, grabbed Grant by the shoulders, shook him out of his trance and pulled him into the garage.

"Well?" Sarah asked Grant. "Are the cats still there?"

Grant nodded, dumbstruck.

"All of them?"

"Looks like a hundred," he said, his voice hollow.

"A hundred?" Natalie said. "Where did they come from?"

"We can't clean a hundred cats," Rudy said.

"Look," Brian said, calm as usual, "they're zombies; they move real slow. Let's just get out there and get it done."

"All right," I said. "Grant, Brian, and I will head out with the first round of soap. Sarah, Natalie, and Rudy, you run out behind us with the brushes. While you're out there scrubbing, we'll get more soap. We'll go back and forth until it's done."

They stared at me, their eyes wide, and I realized I'd bossed them all around. It felt good, I have to say. But I'll be honest. There was a lot of desperation that went into it.

"Don't get bit," I said.

I pulled a box of leather gloves I'd caught sight of earlier from the shelf and handed them out. Sarah opened the case of Joy. Natalie set up the plastic cups on a small patch of the floor not crowded with stuff.

"Oh, no, look," Rudy said. "They're coming."

We watched through the rain as a group of wet, ratty cats limped along the street. We could hear their horrible howling even over the downpour.

"That's not hundreds," I said. And it wasn't. It was just the neighborhood cats. Sarah's seven, my two, Busby, Donald, Silk, and a few others whose names I never knew. We called them each 'Cat.' So...Cat was there. And Cat and Cat. And oh, there was also Cat.

"That is so weird," Natalie said.

"Totally bizarre," Rudy said.

"Crazy," Sarah said.

Cats don't stand around in the rain; do they? Birds, sure. And I've seen a squirrel or two burying acorns in a light rain. But even rodents cower under a bush when it pours; don't they? And the way the cats lumbered awkwardly down the street. Like the night before. Like they had trouble walking straight but it didn't bother them as long as they were getting where they needed to go...eventually. In the pouring rain. No, no. The other little Twits were right—this wasn't normal. The cats were zombies for sure. They had to be, because I'd just thought of my friends as little Twits and didn't even think twice about it.

"Let's do this," Brian said poised at the edge of the line of thick rain pouring off the eaves over the garage. "Grant, stay near me, okay? I'll drag you back if you get stuck."

I felt like we were going into battle.

"I'm okay," Grant said with a nervous smile. "I was surprised before, that's all."

I followed the two of them out to the street, went to the first cat I saw and poured dish soap all over it. It stopped limping, looked up at me and growled. Its red eyes glowed. I stepped away and turned to run back to the garage for more soap. Sarah ran past me, raising her toilet brush into the air, whooping.

"Charge," she called.

110

I laughed; I couldn't help it. Who knew that in the middle of a zombie cat outbreak humor could still be found? It just goes to show there is always something to smile about, no matter how dark the day. No matter how dim the future of civilization. Again and again we ran back and forth, pouring soap all over the cats, batting at them with our toilet brushes in an effort to lather them up. The cats marched up and down the street, soapy and wet. They didn't bother us, but growled and hissed. They came at us once or twice, but didn't chase, once we got several feet from them. Finally, they made their way down the street toward Mr. Haggerty's house.

"They're going back through the hole in the fence, I'll bet," Rudy said.

I shook my head.

"What do you suppose is in Mr. Tanturo's yard?" Brian said. "Do you remember anything weird?"

Back in the garage, soaking wet and shivering, Grant said, "I think they need to eat some squirrel brains or something. Mr. Tanturo's always ranting about the squirrels. So maybe that's it."

"Well, I'd rather they were eating squirrel brains than mine," I said.

"I told you they'd do as much," Brian said. "They know instinctively we're too big. Like the ball python who won't try to strangle a raccoon."

"Could a ball python catch a raccoon?" I said.

"That's not the point," Sarah said, pushing her glasses up, leaving a slab of shiny soap on the bridge of her nose.

"Well," Grant said. "Let's take a look."

We dashed back out in the rain and ran down the street to where the cats were still limping along. They were sudsy and foamy. Soap bubbles played in the street. As the rain continued to splatter on them, they were eventually rinsed clean. But they still lumbered down the street, howling like zombie cats. They did as expected and walked through Mr. Haggarty's yard, disappearing into the wood lot behind it.

Back in the garage, Rudy pulled some towels out of the laundry room and handed them around. The rain was nothing but a sprinkle now.

"I don't think it did anything," I said.

"It was a long shot, after all."

"We don't know yet," Sarah said. "We should wait."

I know it sounds silly, but we all crossed our fingers.

Chapter Twenty-two

We waited three days and thought we'd done it. We'd cured the zombie cat epidemic with 'Lemon Fresh' Joy and discount toilet brushes. Our cats still looked sick—ratty fur they didn't care about cleaning; tongues spending more time hanging out of their mouths than in; meows that sounded like metal grating on metal—but none of them died and that was a pretty good start.

But on the evening of the third day, Sarah found Rudy and me out in the street in front of my house on our skate boards.

"Well," she said, "Leo DiCaprio died."

We ignored her. Naturally.

"Hello," she said. "Leo DiCaprio died!"

"Yeah," Rudy said. "So?"

"He was good in *Inception*," I said.

"Not Leonardo DiCaprio," Sarah said. "Leo DiCaprio. One of my cats. I found him dead in the bushes out front and I waited fifteen minutes and he woke up."

We stopped our boards and stared at her.

"Are you sure he was dead?" Rudy said.

"After all this time, Rudy Albee, and all we've been through, do you really have to ask me that?"

"Sorry."

And that was that. Cats started dying and waking up all over the neighborhood again. We found Grant and Brian and met up with Natalie in the woods by the old oak. We had to figure out what to do next.

"Time for the ax," Grant said.

We all looked at Brian; he had a weird smirk of a smile on his lips.

"We should at least try *Animal Cops* first," Natalie said. She held out her big bag of chips so we could all have some.

"Then we'll be quarantined. And the cats will end up dead, anyway," Sarah said.

She looked at me sideways and I knew what she was thinking. But the more I thought about it, the more I didn't want Brian the Alien to chop of Gnarly and Fletch's heads.

"I don't want to be quarantined," Grant said.

"But say we chop off their heads," Brian said, "and the cops find out. We would be in big trouble if they can't find anything wrong with them in the autopsies."

"Then they can't find out," Grant said.

"Wait, you mean, we could go to jail?" I said.

"Sure," Brian said. "You can't chop off cats' heads. That's cruelty to animals."

"Not if they're zombies," Grant said.

"All right, all right," I said. "That makes things different." They all looked at me. "It really does."

"So, we call *Animal Cops*?"

"That's a television show," I said. "No. We call animal control." I could feel my whole body fall into a depressed slump. "We'll be quarantined."

"And tested, and poked, and prodded," Grant said.

"That's better than arrested," Rudy said.

"We won't get arrested; Brian will."

"Thanks," Brian said.

"Let's keep trying," Natalie said, munching chips.

I got the feeling Natalie, at least, and maybe Grant, too, thought the whole thing was fun...a great way to pass the time that summer.

"What else is there?" I said. My summer was slipping away from me. No beach. No sun and sand. No pool. No condo. No Grandma. No Disney World! Just Bird Place, Rudy, Sarah, and Natalie. I shrugged. Tears were forming in my eyes and I was about to turn and stalk off back home before embarrassing myself when I heard my mother calling. We all walked out of the woods and found my mom standing in the Albee's driveway talking with Mrs. Albee.

"There you are," Mrs. Albee said. "We've been calling."

"Something awful has happened," my mom said.

We all looked at one another knowingly, thinking our parents had finally realized a zombie cat outbreak had hit our neighborhood.

"The cat litter has been recalled," Mrs. Albee said.

"It's been making cats very sick," Mom said. "We need you to go around the neighborhood and get it all back."

"Right now?" I said. "In the dark?"

"Right now, Alfie," Mom said.

"I'm off to the store to buy a different brand to replace it," Mrs. Albee said.

"And you'll take the new litter around when she gets back."

My mom was trying to sound mean, I could tell. But we all smiled and nodded. That was it, then. It was cat litter all the time. They were probably breathing in poison with every swipe of the paw and it was making them sick. They must not have been really dying. Kids do exaggerate, I guess. Even though it sure seemed like they were dead.

We spent all that night dragging bags of cat litter back to the Albee's and then new cat litter out to our neighbors who reported that yes, indeed, their cats had been acting very strangely. Ferrets, too. And Guinea pigs, which don't actually use litter as far as I know. And then I thought of Cow. She'd stopped dying in the last week, but I had to wonder...how could she have come into contact with the cat litter? I surmised that Gnarly, being new to the house and all, must have jumped onto Pearl's desk and got a little too curious about Cow, thus, spreading the cat litter fumes from her paws to the little rodent.

Made sense.

Sort of.

Not really. But I tried to ignore my suspicions. I decided to enjoy the idea that I would get to spend my summer at the beach, after all.

Chapter Twenty-three

Two nights later, I was awake, all by myself, watching television at eleven o'clock when I realized I'd forgot to put the cats out like my mother told me to do before she went to bed. When I searched the house for them, they were nowhere to be found. I'd like to say that was unusual, but it wasn't. Still, I knew all of the hiding places. I checked in the hall closets, on the towel shelf and the shelf where my mom keeps her yarn. One of the cats is usually asleep in one of those spots when they can't be found. But they weren't there. So I looked under my bed. Nope. Then I snuck into Pearl's room and looked under her bed and then on her window sill, even though Gnarly only hid there during the day. Not there.

The only other place I might find them was in my parents' bedroom, on the chair in the corner across from their bed. The last time I tried to sneak into my parents' room at night, I crawled on the floor to the closet with my flashlight in my mouth, hoping to find the stash of Christmas presents. That didn't turn out very well. I didn't realize my mom would think there was a burglar in her bedroom and scream like that.

I had to assume the cats weren't in there. After all, my mom would have tossed them out if they were there when she went to sleep. So, instead, I went out onto the back porch and called for them as quietly as I could. "Kitty, kitty, kitty," I said. Don't laugh. That's how you have to call them. My mom can do it really fast.

When I heard a meow, I looked all over the porch, but didn't find a cat. I heard it again and went out into the back yard. The meow seemed to be moving. So, I followed it. When I got out onto the street, there was Fletch, under the street light, limping and howling. His fur stuck out all over him. He stopped briefly to barf something up, and then continued. I stood there and watched him for a while, not knowing what to do and then I saw Sarah walking up the street.

"Fletch, too?" she said.

"He looks sick."

"All of mine are gone. I'm not even sure how they got out of the house."

"What should we do?"

She shrugged. "Let's go to Mr. Haggarty's and see if they're going out into the woods."

And so we walked over to Rudy's and found him out front too, with his flashlight, looking down the street toward Mr. Haggarty's house. We could see several cats in the dark, crossing the old man's front yard.

"Boo!" Sarah said as we approached, and Rudy jumped.

"The cats have gone complete zombie, now," he said. "I think they're all headed over to Mr. Tanturo's backyard for some kind of zombie cat ritual."

"Like what?" Sarah said.

"I don't know but I don't want to listen to the screaming again. Come on. Let's go out to the oak."

We walked into the woods behind Rudy's house in silence until we came to the oak and sat down under its huge branches.

"Do you think we're going to have to chop off their heads?" Rudy asked.

"Maybe," Sarah said.

"But we'll get in trouble," I said.

"The way I see it," she said, pushing her glasses up her nose. "We have a moral duty to chop them off."

"A moral duty?" Rudy said.

"That's right. The cats are clearly sick. They might even be suffering. But most importantly, they pose a health risk to the neighborhood. Maybe the world."

I shivered.

Rudy nodded. "The world," he said, awestruck.

"*Shh*," Sarah said, putting a hand on my arm. "Do you hear that?"

We were silent for a moment and then I heard it. A low, moaning meow. We turned this way and that.

"Where is it?"

Rudy's flashlight beam danced around the bushes but nothing was there.

"They didn't find any squirrels in Mr. Tanturo's backyard," Rudy cried.

"They're here for us," Sarah screamed. "There!"

I felt something brush against my leg and shouted, "Run!"

So, we ran through the little wood down to Rudy's house and out front, under the streetlight where we stopped, panting; we paced.

"It was the cats," I said shivering, despite the warm

night air.

Sarah nodded. "I saw red eyes glowing in the dark. It was definitely them."

"We have to tell the others," Rudy said.

"But it's after midnight," she said.

"You're darn right it's after midnight," Grant said.

We jumped, startled, and Rudy picked up a rock and threw it at his brother. "You can't come out and start talking like that. Can't you see we're traumatized?"

Grant smiled.

"It's not funny," Sarah said. "The cats nearly attacked us in the woods."

"Cool," Grant said. "Let's get Brian and investigate the situation."

"You want to go back in there?" Rudy said. "Are you crazy?"

"You have a better idea, little twit?"

"We need to tell Mom and Dad. We should all tell our parents."

"I've tried that," I said. "They won't believe us. Every time Gnarly or Fletch gets around my mom they act normal. They even look normal."

"Maybe we're crazy," Rudy said.

"All of us at the same time? I know we're kids, but what are the odds of that?"

"Well," he said. "Maybe it's not a zombie cat virus. Maybe it's a kid virus that makes us think our pets are zombies."

"There's not a virus like that," Grant said. "Is there?"

"Well, my mom would say there's no such thing as a zombie virus," Sarah said.

"But we have evidence," Rudy said.

"Evidence they can't see," I said.

"Then, we're crazy," Rudy said. "Either that or I'm

having a really long dream."

Grant reached out and pinched Rudy hard on the arm.

"*Ow!* What'd you do that for?" He punched his brother on the shoulder.

"You're not dreaming, see?"

Sarah rolled her eyes. "You can get pinched in a dream."

"But it doesn't hurt," I said.

"You don't know," she said. "Anyway, you're not dreaming, Rudy. Why would I be in your dream? If anyone here is dreaming, it's me."

"How do you know?" Rudy said.

"Because I'm here and I know I'm here so I can't be in your dream."

"But how do I know? You could be saying that in my dream."

"Oh, come on. Let's go home and go to bed," I said. "We'll check on the cats tomorrow."

"Wait," Sarah said. "Will you guys walk me home?"

"What for?" I looked at Sarah as she bit her lower lip. "You're scared?"

"What if one of them attacks me? I don't want to be the first of us to get the zombie virus."

"Can't happen," Rudy said.

"How do you know?" Grant said.

"Because you're all figments in my dream."

"I am not," Sarah said. "Oh, forget it." She stomped off across the street.

Rudy and I left Grant in the yard and followed Sarah down Scrub Jay and around to Blue Jay and watched her slip quietly through her front door. Then I turned to Rudy in the dark.

"It wasn't the cat litter," I said.

He nodded.

"I guess we really are going to have to let Brian chop their heads off."

"I just thought of something really awful."

"What?" The skin on my arms tickled with goose bumps.

"What if chopping off their heads doesn't work?"

All that night in bed, I tossed and turned and dreamed of being chased by staggering headless cats and their rolling, thumping heads.

Chapter Twenty-Four

The next morning after my parents left for work, I went to meet everybody out in front of Rudy's house. Even though I'd eaten breakfast, I felt empty and a little bit dizzy. I think it was lack of sleep and this image of Gnarly's head bouncing along the sidewalk toward me, his tongue flapping around like a string. That's not the sort of thing you want to dream about if you need to be alert the next morning. As soon as I came up to the group, they all turned to watch me and I realized I was limping a little. Grant smirked and Brian stared his usual dull stare. But Rudy looked concerned.

Natalie shoved the last bit of a banana in her mouth and said, I think, "I'm not going into the woods."

"We told them about last night," Sarah said.

I looked at Brian and Natalie and nodded. "It's true. I think one of the cats might have bit me on the leg."

"What?" Sarah's eyes flew open wide. "Why didn't you say so last night?"

"It might have just brushed up against me. But I don't know."

They made me pull up my jeans to show them my leg and there weren't any teeth marks in my skin. Still, somehow, overnight, I found myself sure I'd been bitten. Funny how fear works on you.

"Well, that's it," Grant said. "We've tried everything I can think of. You guys got any other ideas?"

We all looked at one another, shaking our heads.

"You're going to have to admit it," he said. "It's time to chop off their heads. You got an ax, Brian?"

Brian shrugged.

"That's okay. You can use ours. Let's see if we can find the cats. Is Busby home?"

Rudy shook his head. We all stood there for a few seconds longer, maybe trying not to move forward in time. I was starting to think my summer at the condo was gone, either way. I was either going to be a zombie, or eaten by one, or I was going to jail for chopping off my neighbors' cats' heads.

"There has to be another way," I mumbled. But I knew there wasn't. We had to save the neighborhood. We had to save the world.

"How can we chop off the heads of other people's cats?" Natalie said as we started walking down the street.

"It's an awful business," Grant said. "But somebody's got to do it. And Brian's just that somebody."

"We're going to jail for sure," Rudy said.

"Just Brian," Sarah said.

"We'll all testify for him," I said. "We'll say he had to do it. He's a hero."

We walked around the whole neighborhood but

couldn't find our cats anywhere.

"Oh, no," Rudy said. "It just occurred to me."

"What?" I said.

"They've been going through the hole in the fence."

"Yeah, so?" Grant said.

"They may have already infected other cats...outside our neighborhood."

"It may be too late," Sarah said.

"Doesn't matter," Grant said. "We have to chop off as many heads as we can. We have to try."

And suddenly, that image of Gnarly's head rolling and bumping along chasing me turned into an image of thousands of cat heads, filling the streets of the city, howling and hissing, their crazy tongues flapping against the asphalt with every revolution.

"All right," Rudy said. "They seem to be coming out at night and going through the fence. We'll meet up under the oak as soon as it gets dark."

After Brian and Grant went inside Rudy's house, Rudy turned to the rest of us and said, "Sometimes I think Grant just wants to see Brian chop off their heads."

"Your brother is so weird," Natalie said.

"I'm going back to bed," I said.

"How can you sleep at a time like this?" Natalie said.

She was right. I couldn't sleep. I tried, but it was no use. When my mom came home for lunch, she asked me all sorts of questions and was a little perturbed at me for grunting at most of them.

"Is everything okay?" she finally said.

And, probably because I was basically walking in my sleep, I said, "The cats are zombies and we're going to have to chop off their heads."

She smiled, left the table, put her plate into the dishwasher, and said, "That's good. Fresh air is the best medicine."

And then she went back to work.

After dinner, I headed out slightly before sunset. I tried to tell myself it was because I was bored and still tired and didn't have anything better to do. But I'm pretty sure the truth of it was that I didn't want to walk out into the woods all by myself in the dark. Best to get there in daylight, by the familiar old oak, and wait for everybody else to show up. But as I walked the path, it occurred to me that if everybody was late, I'd be standing out in the woods all by myself in the dark. I shuddered.

When I left the path and looked to the oak, I saw Brian the Alien and stopped. He saw me come off the path or I would have turned and left. Instead, I stood there like a dork for a few seconds too long, until he finally stopped waiting for me to walk over and said, "How's it going?"

"It, uh, fine," I said. Total dork.

"I saw one of the neighbors' cats, next door to Grant. It was one I sprayed with cortisone. I felt bad."

He frowned and for some odd reason that prompted my feet to move. I walked over and sat on the dirt under the tree. He sat, too.

"What for?" I said.

He shrugged. "It was like, I don't know. Cats like me. Do they like you?"

"Like me? I guess."

"Well, they like me a lot. All of my friends' cats like me. They get up on my lap and let me pet them. My friends are always saying how their cats don't act like that with other people."

"That's cool, I guess."

126

"Yeah."

"So, you saw one?" I don't know if it was because I didn't get any sleep the night before, but I wasn't sure what the Alien was trying to say.

"He looked at me like I'd betrayed him."

I nodded, still not completely getting it.

"I betrayed his trust."

We were quiet for a few seconds too long and it started to feel weird. So, I said, "You don't seem like the kind of person cats would like."

"Why's that?"

I was pretty busy freaking out, my eyes were open so wide the whites were going to dry up. I couldn't believe I'd said that and now he wanted me to explain why. "I don't know," I said trying to think up some kind of excuse. Instead, my mouth went on without me. "You're kind of scary...I mean...to children. So, yeah, maybe pets, too." If I could have smacked myself in the head without really looking weird, I would have.

"It's the eyes, isn't it?" he said.

"Huh?"

"Why you guys are afraid of me. You think I'm weird. And violent. A monster or something. Those stories. They aren't true, you know? It's all made up. Because of the eyes."

I just stared at him, his huge eyes magnified through his lenses, ogling me. I realized I was staring at the very thing he was talking about so I jerked my gaze away from his.

"*Nah*," I said. "We don't think you're weird."

"You call me an alien," he said.

Dang it. Can't anybody keep secrets? One of the little Twits squealed and I was going to have to find out who–or whom. Mrs. Wilkinson would know which word is correct. It was not cool. You can leak out good stuff, like if Rudy liked a girl or something. But you don't leak out bad things we say about people. That's just not nice.

"We didn't mean it." Weak excuse.

"It's okay. My mom—well, she does crafts. Does your mom do crafts?"

I shook my head. My mom worked full time and spent her weekends at luncheons and lectures.

"Well, my mom's really into them. She takes these shells—she says she's making Florida crafts, but these shells are like, clam shells and I don't know if they have clams in Florida."

"Sure they do. Right out there in the lagoon."

"Really?"

He turned to me again with a little smile on his face. An odd feeling coursed through me. He was like... a neighborhood legend. Brian. The Alien. The man with the eyes. Man being the main word there. He was older and smarter. He drove a car and dated girls. And he was talking to me like he thought I was just like him.

"So, she glues these big plastic eyes to these clam shells and the black pupils inside wiggle. She calls them googly eyes."

I looked at him. "So?"

"That's what I am. I'm a little face, with two enormous googly eyes."

I looked him full in the face and laughed. I laughed loud and hard. I couldn't stop laughing and he started laughing, too. We held our stomachs and rocked back and forth and I fell against the trunk of the oak, then over onto my side and tears rolled down my face. Finally we started making long sighing noises between our guffaws and eventually we quieted down, except every once in a while a giggle would escape.

Brian sighed then, and frowned. "I can't do it," he

said.

"Do what?"

"I can't kill the cats. I can't chop off their heads. Can't do it."

I sat for a while realizing over and over again that Brian wasn't an alien at all. He was just a goofy looking older kid we liked to tell stories about. It was going to take a little while to sink in completely.

"Yeah," I said. "I wouldn't be able to do it, either."

It was dark now and we heard voices, but they weren't coming from the path. Instead, they echoed down the way, in the direction of Mr. Haggerty's house. And suddenly, Sarah burst through the shrubs, panting, a look of shock on her face.

Chapter Twenty-Five

Hurry," she said. "The cats are in the neighborhood, on the streets. Grant and Rudy are over at the hole in the fence. We're going to go through and see what's going on."

I was against it, for a lot of reasons. But Brian got up and followed Sarah, running through the woods. So, what else could I do? When we got to the hole, Rudy had already gone through. The rest of us crawled into Mr. Tanturo's yard one by one. We stood, and stared, trying to make out what we were seeing with only the moon and a porch light two doors down to see by.

Two cats were pawing at and chewing on something under Mr. Tanturo's big oak tree.

"What is it?" I said.

Grant walked forward, reached down and picked something up. The cats meowed, deep and freakishly, and followed him, howling, as he carried it over to us.

"What is it?" I said again.

"Oh, my flash light," Rudy said.

He dug his light out of his jeans pocket and flicked it on.

There were four seconds of silence as we all looked at what Grant was holding and then we screamed and ran, and clambered over one another on the ground, trying to get back through the hole. We ran like wild animals. Brian was in the lead and I followed. He was going for the oak, which I thought was a bad idea, but was in no position to argue. We ran. And we screamed. Natalie overtook me, shrieking like she was being attacked, and I sped up. I did not want to be the last one.

It was a squirrel. A dead, rotted, chewed on squirrel. And when we all stopped and walked in circles at the old oak, we realized Grant brought it with him. He held it up again with a big smile on his face.

"Shine the light again," he said and Rudy did so. "Look, its little head is smashed in and its brains are gone."

"*Ahhhh*," Sarah said and danced around, brushing imaginary bugs off her. "Cut it out. *Ew*." She shivered from head to foot.

"Can I pet it?" Natalie said, reaching out for the tail.

"Are you out of your mind?" I said, swatting her hand down. "You could get rabies."

"I'm pretty sure the animal has to bite you to get rabies," she said. "Isn't that right, Brian?"

"It's transmitted through bites and scratches. The skin has to be penetrated. And the virus has to be a-live."

"Nothing's left alive in that," Rudy said.

"I think it's better to be safe than sorry," Brian said. "And the standard rule is not to touch dead animals. So..."

We stood around looking at Grant, who was still smiling.

"But don't you see?" he said. "The cats were eating it."

"Our cats have rabies?" Natalie said. "From squirrels?"

"Could be," Brian said. "Or the zombie virus is in the squirrels."

Sarah started hitting my arm and I brushed her off. "Cut it out," I said. But she only slapped harder until I looked at her. Her eyes were as big as my mom's snicker doodle cookies, her mouth was open and she was staring into the woods. We all turned to look and there were a dozen cats, sitting in a clump, their tongues hanging out of their mouths and their eyes glassy and pinkish.

Meowwwrrr, they started singing. *Meeeeowwwrrr*.

"They came for their squirrel," Grant said.

"Well, give it back to them," Brian said.

I'd never in my life heard Brian the Alien panicked and the sound of fear in his voice sent shivers all over me. My heart pounded and Natalie jumped and let out a shriek. I turned, and there were more cats behind us, purring so loud it sounded like a semi-truck on the highway.

Meoooowwwrrr, they demanded.

"Throw it!" Sarah screamed. She pushed Grant forward, toward one of cat hives.

He tossed the squirrel, but it was too late. The cats were after us. They screamed and hissed and growled and we ran. Straight through the woods. Forget the path. We ran around trees, into and over shrubs, against the saw palmettos and brambleberry bushes. And all the time the cats shrieked and chased us and I couldn't tell if I was being attacked by them or by thorns and palmetto teeth.

Sarah screamed. Natalie wailed. Rudy shouted. Grant shrieked. I think I was bawling. And Brian the Alien? Brian the Alien was laughing and yelling and laughing and yelling, like a maniac.

We ran through Rudy's yard and down Scrub Jay to Sand Hill Road. We ran all the way to Ibis, down to the dead end, through the empty lot over to Blue Jay, down to Sarah's house, through her yard and over to Sea Gull. And the cats chased us the whole way.

"I thought you said zombie cats were slow," Sarah said, out of breath.

"Who made me the expert on zombies?" Brian said.

"I have an idea," Grant said, huffing and puffing. "This way."

"Oh, please," Rudy screamed as he ran. "Since when have you ever had a good idea?"

"Trust me."

We really had no choice. We couldn't run in circles in the neighborhood all night. We couldn't go inside somebody's house. How would we ever escape?

"We have to fix this now," I said.

"We will," Grant said. "I know exactly what to do."

And so we followed him, down to the end of Sea Gull and over to Scrub Jay again. Back down the street, past Rudy's house, over to Mr. Haggerty's, through his yard and through the woods out back to the hole in the fence.

"Hurry!" Grant shouted. "Through the hole."

"What?" I balked.

"Just do it."

The others were doing as they were told and even though I had my doubts–really, really big ones–I crawled through. Grant came through after us and said,

"Don't let them through the hole. I'll be right back."

We stood there, aghast. Aghast, I tell you!

"How are we supposed to keep them out?" Rudy yelled at his brother in the dark.

We heard him far away, probably out front of Mr. Tanturo's house. "Somebody will have to sacrifice himself."

Nobody volunteered. But Sarah knelt and peered through the hole.

"They're coming!"

Grant showed up finally with a lid from a trash can and shoved it up against the hole.

"There," he said. He sat down and leaned against the lid, holding it in place.

"There what?" Rudy said.

"We're safe." Grant grinned.

"What are we supposed to do now?" Natalie said.

"Hey," Grant said. "I did the hard part."

The little Twits looked at Brian. I don't know about the rest of them, but I was about ready to cry. Brian had to help us. We could hear the cats beyond the fence, meowing. More and more of them were gathering. When Mr. Tanturo's backyard lit up, we all jumped and turned to see the old man standing on his back porch, the porch light making us squint.

"What's going on out here?" Mr. Tanturo said.

There was silence for a second or two, except for the howling of all our cats behind the fence, and then we all started explaining at once. We went on for some time. Cats dying and coming back and tongues flapping around and dreams of cat heads chasing me and zombies and squirrels and Cow, the hamster, and running. Finally, our voices trickled down to nothing and Mr. Tanturo tilted his head this way and then that.

"They were eating a dead squirrel, you say?"

"Yes, sir," Brian said.

Mr. Tanturo came toward us and looked to the ground underneath his big oak tree. "Are you sure they weren't eating that?"

We went over to the oak and looked down. There, on a plastic dish, were bits of what looked like cookies.

"What is it?" Grant said, still sitting against the trash can lid at the fence. "Tell me."

"What is it, Mr. Tanturo?" I said.

"I didn't mean any harm," the old man said. "I was only trying to keep your darn squirrels away. I didn't mean to kill any of them. Just make them a little sick. As a warning. You know?"

"But what is it?"

"That there is a toxic concoction, baked into muffins."

"What's in it?" Brian asked him.

"Well," the old man pulled at his chin. "It's got all the things I thought might ward off rodents. Onions, garlic, chocolate–because I hear that's bad for animals–coffee. I figured the coffee would drive them nuts." He laughed. "Nuts. Get it?"

We stared at the broken muffin pieces.

"And I soaked the baked muffins in whiskey. And rolled them in raw eggs after that."

Mr. Tanturo beamed at us. Proud of himself.

"That is a veritable smorgasbord of foods poisonous to cats," Brian said.

"Oh, dear."

"But why would our cats want to eat it?" Sarah said. "It sounds gross."

"Could be the tuna," Mr. Tanturo said. "I thought the tuna would be appealing to the squirrels. It's all mixed in there."

The cats meowed and howled and we all looked at

136

Mr. Tanturo. Finally, he said, "I'll just take it away, now."

We watched as he picked up the dish and walked back inside his house. Then he popped his head out and said, "I reckon your gray squirrels aren't all that bad."

I was going to tell Mr. Tanturo that all the squirrels in Florida are gray squirrels, but he was gone and the porch light flicked off and we were standing in his backyard in the dark again.

"Do you think that's it?" Rudy said.

"Could it be?" Sarah said.

"Well, I'd be sick if I ate that stuff," Natalie said.

"It's a definite possibility," Brian said. "All of those things make cats sick. The whiskey can even induce comas...which would look like death, after all."

I shook my head. "But Cow," I said. "Pearl's hamster didn't eat any of that stuff."

We all stood there, our faces pinched with worry, until Brian coughed and said, "That's a mystery."

"I'll believe it when I see it," I said. "When the cats stop chasing us. And when they stop dying."

Brian nodded at me, as if I'd said something very smart and I couldn't help feel like his equal. "That's right," he said. "Time will tell."

"Wait," Grant said. "Do you hear that?"

Chapter Twenty-six

It was quiet. Eerie. Grant started to move but Rudy stopped him.

"Wait," he said. "They could be on the other side of the fence, waiting for us."

"Here," Brian said. "On my shoulders."

He stooped down and Rudy climbed aboard. Brian stood and Rudy grabbed the top of the wood fence and peered over.

"Well?" I said.

"It's dark."

"Your flashlight, little twit," Grant said. "Why do you always forget your flashlight?"

Rudy managed to pull his little light from his pocket and surveyed the area beyond the fence.

"They're gone."

"It could be a trap," Sarah said as Rudy climbed off Brian's shoulders.

"Cats aren't smart enough to set a trap," I said.

"Cats are very smart," Natalie said.

"Oh, come on," I said. "They didn't set a trap."

"They've probably calmed down is all," Brian said. "We should be able to get home safely. And then tomorrow...we'll see."

We walked through the woods, shaky, on edge, ready to jump and run. But the cats didn't come after us. Grant and Rudy walked everybody to their houses so nobody would have to be alone. My parents were up, in the family room watching television, laughing at something. Pearl was in her room playing with Cow. I ate some chips in the kitchen and then told Mom and Dad I didn't feel well and went to bed. I paced in the dark of my room for a long time before finally feeling like I could sleep.

Over the next week, no cats died. Their tongues managed to stay in their mouths and they started cleaning themselves a lot better. Gnarly still rolled around in the dirt in the gutter, but he shook it off pretty well afterward. The cats still got together and wandered the neighborhood at night, so Grant and Brian boarded up the hole in the fence. Mr. Tanturo said we could climb over anytime we wanted to take the shortcut to the convenience store.

On my last day before I would go to spend two weeks at my gram's condo, I met up with The Twits out by the old oak. Brian and Grant were there, brainstorming an idea for a lift that would get everyone over the fence easier than climbing.

"Why don't we put in a gate?" I said.

Brian smiled at me and punched me lightly in the arm. "What's the fun of that?"

"I guess it's over," Rudy said. He plopped down on the dirt under the oak. "Busby's looking healthier than ever."

"Do you ever wonder, though," Sarah said. "If we

imagined a lot of it?"

"Yes," Natalie said. "What are the odds they could get comas and then just...not be in a coma, anymore?"

"True enough," Brian said.

I turned to Rudy. "But you said Busby was flat as a spit splat."

"A split splat?" Sarah said.

"Spit splat," I corrected.

"Sphlit sphalt," she tried again.

"A split–I mean, a spit splat. You know...spit."

Rudy shook his head. "I hate to say it, but after what we've been through, everything is a little blurry. I was so sure, though. So sure."

"So," I said, "it's possible. There could have been a zombie cat outbreak. And maybe something we did cured it. We just don't know."

We all stood there, nodded, maybe awed, possibly terrified.

And Brian said, "We may never know for sure."

Natalie said, "Spit splat spit splat split splat splat splat split."

That night, I lay in bed trying to sleep, worried. I wondered if Brian Watley was worried, too. What if there had been a zombie cat outbreak and what if the cats weren't cured? He couldn't chop off their heads, and I knew I couldn't do it. What would we do? What would the future hold?

When I felt something crawling on the blanket over my legs, I froze. I was–and I'm not exaggerating–paralyzed with fear. It was Gnarly or Fletch for sure, come to bore their sharp little teeth into my skull and eat my brains. The zombie cat apocalypse was real, I thought. It was here. And I was lying there letting it happen. But, when the creature scampered onto my chest, I knew it couldn't be a cat. I reached over and flicked on the lamp.

"Cow?"

Pearl's hamster was sniffing, his whiskers twitching, and padding all over my blanket. I scooped him up and snuck into Pearl's room to return him to his cage. I thought his eyes were a little pink in the light from the hallway. But it could have been my imagination. When I closed Pearl's door behind me, there in the hall, staring at me, his eyes glowing red, was Fletch.

I choked out a laugh. "Uh, hiya there, buddy. Fletch."

He stood on all fours, meowed, then turned and walked into the darkness of the living room. All that night I wondered about it. Cow was out of his cage and Fletch didn't even know it—didn't try to eat him. And his eyes. They were red. Glowing red.

I left the next morning for my grandmother's condo, feeling like I was making an escape. And leaving my friends behind to face the zombie cat apocalypse.

Dianna Dann Narciso writes in a variety of genres under several pen names. Her books include:

Children's chapter books:
Wayward Cat Finds a Home by Dana Trantham

Middle-grade fiction:
Zombie Cats by Dana Trantham

Fantasy by Dana Trantham:
Children of Path: The Kell Stone Prophecy Book One
The Wretched: The Kell Stone Prophecy Book Two

Story Runners: Awakening

Coming in 2015
The Kell Stone Prophecy Book Three
The Kell Stone Prophecy: Complete Trilogy

Paranormal humor:
Zombie Revolution by D.D. Charles

Literary fiction:
Camelia by Dianna Dann
Always Magnolia by Dianna Dann

For more information about the author and Wayward Cat Publishing, visit:

waywardcatpublishing.com
diannadann.com

Made in the USA
Columbia, SC
10 September 2017